D0108296

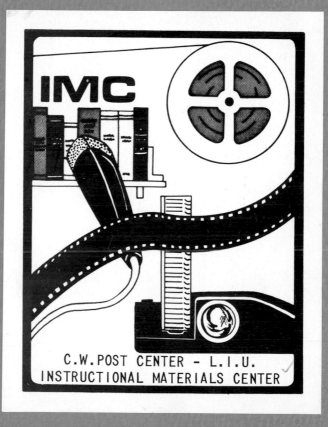

C.W. POST CENTER - L.I.U.
INSTRUCTIONAL MATERIALS CENTER

The Girl Who
Had No Name

Other books
by Berniece Rabe

NAOMI
RASS

The Girl Who Had No Name

BY BERNIECE RABE

E. P. DUTTON | NEW YORK

Library of Congress Cataloging in Publication Data

Rabe, Berniece   The girl who had no name

SUMMARY: As she travels from sister to sister in
search of a home after the death of their mother, a
twelve-year-old country girl discovers many things
about herself and her family, including why she was
never given a name at birth.

[1. Family life—Fiction.   2. Country life—Fiction]
I. Title.
PZ7.R105Gi [Fic]   76–56768   ISBN 0–525–30660–9

Published simultaneously in Canada by Clarke,
Irwin & Company Limited, Toronto and Vancouver

Editor: Ann Durell
Designer: Meri Shardin
Printed in the U.S.A.   First Edition
10 9 8 7 6 5 4 3 2 1

Dedicated to
my husband, Walter,
who started me writing

one

THE whispering was driving Girlie crazy. She'd turned twelve in April of this year, 1936, and twelve was plenty old enough to be spoken out loud to, like a thinking member of the family. She was not a child! Even among the whispers that fact had been confirmed when people said, "It's a blessing that Mary lived to raise her girls. Be thankful she left no little 'uns."

But then the voices would lower and eyes would be cautious lest she come close to them and hear the rest, just as if she were a "little 'un."

It was torment. It was enough to drive her out of the house, away from everyone. She left her sisters Nita and Darnella, who were an acceptable fourteen and sixteen, to continue their whispering with Wanda, the still older sister who was married and lived in St. Louis. As she headed past Wanda's little Susy, she saw the child was playing with Papa's Prince Albert tobacco.

"Here, Susy, that ain't for little girls."

Girlie stuffed the tobacco can into her dress pocket. She took a step to one side to pick up the cigarette papers too. Quickly she left the house and headed for the barn, stopping only once long enough to pick up her cat, Clark Gable. She draped him over one shoulder, and he clung on while she climbed into the barn loft.

Clark Gable found a place in the sun by the big center opening where the hay was hoisted in. But Girlie chose a place farther back before she spread her lap wide to accommodate the tobacco and papers, and began rolling a cigarette. Papa could roll one with two flicks of his fingers and a fast lick of his tongue to make the paper end stick. But Girlie kept spilling the tobacco out of the paper. Finally she unpinned the little white-handled knife that Papa had given her. She always wore it on her belt.

A couple of probes with the knife and she was able to make some of the tobacco stay down inside the cigarette. She climbed down the ladder and got one of the matches Papa kept tucked in a crack of timber next to the lantern in the horse's stall. But she hadn't taken two puffs back in the loft when Nita was there, standing quietly, her mouth pursed into a smart accusing set.

"Well, well. Mama always said that with nine girls there was a fair chance that one of us might take up Papa's bad habit. It ought to make Mama real proud at what you're doing, and her not dead two months."

"Mama died June fourth, so she's been dead two months and two days," Girlie said. "You can't even figure right!"

"Girlie! I'm telling Papa that you're smoking."

"Won't do no good. Papa don't care what any of us does anymore. Anyway, he smokes."

"I didn't say he didn't. Mama always tried to get him to give it up, so he wouldn't kill himself. He wouldn't believe her, but even Papa hates to see a woman smoking. He'll do something about it; you wait and see."

Nita was right. She was sassy and prissy and right . . . and she was climbing down the ladder on her way to tell Papa. Quickly Girlie put out her cigarette and ran to get her.

She caught Nita midway across the yard; grabbed her, and wrestled her down with a thud into the sandy soil. Nita didn't lie still for a second. She was a fighter. That was all right. Girlie felt like fighting. She felt like fighting the whole world. She had finally managed to get Nita pinned to the ground just as Wanda came running and scolding.

"Cut that out! Girlie, you let Nita up right this minute. Come on, move. Get up and dust that sand off your dresses." Girlie allowed Wanda to jerk Nita free and up. Wanda began vigorously trying to dust every speck of sand off Nita's dress.

Girlie said, "You're wasting your time. Mama says Southeast Missouri sand can't ever be completely dusted off."

As she quoted Mama, her voice got tight, and she suddenly missed Mama something furious. What had she done? She'd started smoking, the very thing Mama had warned them not to do.

Wanda stopped the dusting at last and demanded, "What's this fighting all about?"

Now Nita had a wide-open invitation to tattle and did. Girlie let her spill out the whole story and only groaned from the weight of it all. "Oh-h-h, I'll never be what Mama wanted me to be."

Wanda touched her shoulder. "Come on, both you girls. Let's go in the house. Girlie, you got lots of time to be what Mama wanted."

Nita moved close to Wanda, and by the time they had all reached the back door, Nita was hugged against her side, as if she were the one who needed comforting. There was a smell on the back porch, worse than the usual smell of table slop.

Girlie said, "Nita didn't wash the bean pot last night."

Wanda's arm moved from Nita's waist. "What? Well, where is it? Why, in this hot weather the leaving's will be soured."

Girlie nodded. "It is soured. It's worse than soured, it's crudded over with mold. Mama'd die if she knew that Nita let that bean pot get moldy. Nita promised Darnella she'd wash it."

"You liar," Nita said angrily. "I told Darnella to go on and have fun with Galen, and I'd wash the dishes, but I didn't promise to wash that heavy old iron bean pot. You're a lying little brat!"

"I'm not a liar! I try very hard not to tell lies, and I think I'm doing well for a beginner."

But she had lied. It was true that Darnella had said dishes and not bean pot. Her old habit of failing to mention some of the facts or mixing them up a bit to fit whatever she cared to state had gotten in the way of truth again. Mama had scolded her about this, and she had not done it once since Mama died. She felt terrible for doing it now, but that was none of Nita's business. "Leave me alone," she shouted. "And don't call me *little*. I'll be in eighth grade next year."

Nita crumpled into a tight little bent-over thing and began to sob. With Mama dead, Nita, who had graduated from eighth grade in June, would not be continuing school. Papa had said it was out of the question.

Girlie couldn't yell anymore at a body who was crying. She walked into the living room. There was Papa, down on the floor pulling funny faces to make Susy laugh, just the way he used to play with Girlie. But the minute he saw her, he stopped and stood up.

"Girlie, find my tobacco! I want it by the time me and Galen turn in from work tonight."

Papa left at once for the melon patch, and Girlie raced out to the barn loft to get the tobacco and to be near someone who cared. Clark Gable was still sunning. His fur was warm and soft and comforting.

"Oh, Clark, what's come over Papa? Do you suppose he heard me yelling at Nita? Why do I have such a temper? I ought to control myself, even if Nita does provoke me. Calling me 'little'!" Smack! Girlie hit a bale of hay with her flattened hand. It scared Clark Gable. He jumped to the top of the stack of bales.

Since Papa had no sons to help him in the fields, he had to buy hay rather than raise his own. Papa complained of being cursed by bearing ten daughters and no sons, yet he wouldn't let a one of the girls do a man's work. Girlie thought Papa would profit by at least letting her help with the business side of things. She could begin by writing down the melon orders, which she would do far better than Darnella. Why, in no time at all, she'd have him selling melons directly to the city while she stayed home and took care of the farm. In St. Louis, he'd stand to sell the biggest cantaloupes for ten cents *each*. Quickly she took out her school fountain pen from her pocket and began to calculate the profits. She had to write on her thighs, since she had no paper.

5

It seemed she'd have them making fifty dollars in no time. She wished he'd at least let her try to help in some way. Why, anyone could just look at her hands and know she could be of help. She had big hands, the widest hand-span of anyone in school, and that included the boys. She flexed her fingers and stared at them. Her hands were pretty in spite of their size. Her fingers were long and slim, but the tissues between the knuckles were more flexible than other people's. It was one more way she looked different from the other girls. Nita said she was part duck and part crow. Well, she liked her hands the way they were and she couldn't help that her hair was darker than the others.

She really wished she had smacked Nita. She hit the hay again and again and again. Take that for calling me a liar, and that for being so goody-good about smoking, and that for. . . . She beat the bale until she was exhausted.

She laid her head on the bale of green hay, inhaled its grassy smell, and drifted into a nice dream. She was running a happy household for Papa. Papa was proud of her and told all the neighbors, "Mama trained Girlie so well, she just carried on nice and easy when she passed on."

The smell of smoke awoke her. Over in the far corner of the barn loft rose a small whirling, swirling puff of smoke. It was a whirling mess because Nita was right in the middle of it, coughing and stamping the smoldering bale of hay.

"Girlie, wake up and move! Help me get this out!"

Nita seemed to be doing a fair job of putting it out. Still Girlie climbed up to get Clark Gable and toss him to safety out of the big loft opening. He landed catlike on all

6

four feet and stalked huffily away. Nita was still stamping, and now seemed to be fanning the fire into flames rather than putting it out.

"Nita, was you smoking too?" The thought was shocking but there Nita was, and how else could a fire have started?

"Me?" Nita was coughing. "Me? Why you . . . you're the one that left that cigarette butt here to smolder and start a fire. I was just out here trying to find that hen's nest."

"I'll get some water," Girlie said.

She tucked her dress between her knees and slid down the hay-hoist rope to the pig's slop pail. She scooped it full of water from the horse's watering trough, hooked it onto the rope, and yelled, "Hoist!"

Nita was still coughing but nonetheless the pail started to move loftward, and Nita had it. A puff of smoke gushed out from the loft, and a hen, cackling and fluttering her wings, came sailing out in the midst of it.

"It's out. The fire's out," Nita yelled. "Catch the slop pail, Girlie."

Girlie caught the pail and removed it from the rope. Then she shinnied back up the rope to join Nita. Nita's shoes were black with char, but the smoke was settling and the fire was indeed out.

"Nita! Girlie! You all right?" Wanda and Darnella were yelling from below.

Girlie said, "Sure, we're all right. The fire's out. I told Galen to get us dry hay, not that green stuff that was bound to cause spontaneous combustion."

Girlie walked to the barn opening and saw that Galen was standing there beside Darnella. She wished she hadn't said what she did. She had told Galen about the hay, but she was not telling Wanda the real facts about how the fire started. She'd done it again, twisting the truth. She let out a moan.

Nita whispered firmly into her ear, "Girlie, I ain't going to tell Wanda you're lying if you promise never to smoke again. Will you promise?"

"It ain't any of your business, Nita. I thank you for putting out the fire, but it ain't any of your business. I'm going to be someone Papa can be proud of, not someone to please Miss High-and-Mighty Nita Webster!" Girlie slid back down the rope and Nita came down the ladder.

Wanda began shouting, "Nita, look at your shoes. Papa'll kill you!"

At the same moment Darnella reached for Girlie and cried, "Oh, Girlie, honey, your legs, you've burned your legs!"

"Darnella, put my dress tail down. Galen's standing right there. I ain't burned. That's not burns." Girlie forced her dress down to a decent level.

Wanda came over and pulled her dress up again and let out a sigh of relief and consternation. "Girlie, is that ink you've marked all over your legs? Wash it off. Nita, wash your shoes. I tell you, I'm going to end up on Sand Hill right next to Mama if you girls. . . ."

Wanda joined Galen and Darnella, who had already started back to the house.

Girlie joined Nita at the watering trough and quickly began smudging the ink on her thighs. It wasn't an easy job to do if her dress was going to be pulled down decent. It looked like things were settling when Nita suddenly started crying again.

"I'm sorry, Nita. I hate it that your shoes got all black. Is it coming off?"

"It ain't my shoes. I'm crying about Mama being buried all alone up there on Sand Hill."

"It's what everyone is whispering about, ain't it, Nita?"

"Yes," Nita whispered.

"It was because of the dreadful disease Mama had that killed her, wasn't it? That's why Papa buried her in that old worn-out graveyard. No one has been buried on Sand Hill except for Mr. Tellmount, who died of blood poison, and they didn't want him in the regular graveyard. They say he was awful. They didn't even shave him. They just tipped him off his bed into a pine box and buried him fast. But they let us see Mama. Mama looked real pretty in her gold dress. That was a nice color with her dark hair. Didn't you think that was a nice color, Nita? I'd like a dress of. . . ."

Nita had stopped crying and was standing there now, acting as if Girlie had done something wrong again. "How could you Girlie? Talking about clothes when. . . . Oh, I wish I'd have died when Mama had me. She almost died then. She didn't have no disease, Girlie. It was something still wrong from her having me and you . . . oh, I wish I was dead, too."

"Well, I don't. I know Mama almost died when I was born, but I don't talk like that. I'm glad I was born . . . and I'm glad I'm not dead and buried up on Sand Hill. Mama told us to always set our minds on good things. . . . Nita, why did Papa bury Mama on Sand Hill if she didn't have a dread disease? No one else gets buried there."

"There's been another man buried up there besides Mr. Tellmount. Mr. Garner was buried there."

Girlie didn't like Nita trying to give excuses when there was a thing to be solved. A person never solves a problem by running away from it with excuses. "Nita,

Mr. Garner was an atheist, and said he didn't want his bones rotting with all the hypocrite Christians he'd been forced to live around all his life. You know very good and well that Mama was no atheist. Why did Papa put her up there with strangers? I've got a right to know."

"I don't know myself, Girlie. Stop hollering at me. She ain't with strangers. She's right besides her grandparents. Papa said she liked their grave spot."

"But I still say it ain't natural. Why ain't she with her little Janey which was her second born, and that she's cried over more than once, and her being dead twenty-eight years. She'd have wanted to be buried next to Janey. I know she would!"

Nita didn't answer, she just walked away. Nita's shoes didn't look too bad. Most all the char washed right off. She'd get them dirtier walking out of the barn lot, not watching her step, than she had putting out the fire. That was Nita, walking away instead of trying to stay there and really pool their information, so they could solve this thing about Mama.

Lots of people walked away when Girlie started asking too many questions. She had only one dear friend who was always there. She reached down to stroke the fur of Clark Gable, who was twining himself around her wet legs.

Clark was more human than some people. Maybe it was because she'd found him in a movie theater. He was just a scrawny little black and white kitten then, and Rose, her sister who'd paid for the movie treat, had been mad at Girlie for picking up what she called a homely animal. Girlie never ever had been sorry. As special as the treat to see a real moving picture was, it wasn't one millionth as special as finding Clark Gable.

10

"Clark, if you needed to solve a problem, wouldn't you start looking for facts?"

Somehow, some way she was going to find out what had come over Papa to make him turn mean and distant, and why he'd buried Mama up on Sand Hill.

two

IN her effort to find facts, Girlie took to standing close to Wanda and Darnella when they whispered. She didn't feel wrong in doing so. Papa had always admonished her, "Keep your eyes and ears open and you'll learn enough to get by."

So it was a right and true thing she was doing to listen, but she heard nothing of importance. Darnella was forever kind and never said a bad word about anybody. Her whispers were of love and wanting to date now that she'd turned sixteen. So it was hard to believe it was Darnella talking when one day she heard loud rumbles of angry words from the front room.

"I'm going to tell that son of a gun!"

As quickly as she could, Girlie ran downstairs. Wanda was saying, "You should never have tried to reason with Papa, not yet, not yet, Dar. . . ." She stopped when she saw Girlie, and continued ever so pleasantly, "Darnella, I don't see why we can't kill two or three of them young pullets for dinner. They're big enough."

Girlie didn't care to have the subject changed. "Darnella, what did Papa do now?"

Wanda said, "Girlie, go make them beds upstairs."

"I already did."

"Then make them over. You never take time to fluff the feather tick. You know Mama would want you to make them right."

At the mention of carrying on as Mama would have her, Girlie did weaken and took three steps toward the stairs, but Darnella called her back.

"Stay right where you are, Girlie! You've got to learn sooner or later what kinds of people is in this world. My big trouble was that I learned later, and it's still shocking every time that . . . that . . . maybe you'd better leave the room after all. It puts a strain on me not to call Papa what he is. I'm going to tell him right to his face what he is. I'm going to tell him tomorrow. It ain't human to have to put up with the likes of him. Wanda, I lost my Mama, too. Don't that ever occur to no one? I lost my Mama, too!"

"Of course you did, Darnella. We all miss her. But that don't give you call to let out angry feelings. Mama always said the virtue of a woman is her controlling herself. Girlie, you been wanting to make some pudding for a long time. Why don't you go make us some chocolate pudding. Papa likes your cooking. Go on, run along now."

Girlie hated to stay and listen when Wanda had asked her point blank to leave. Besides, she wanted very much to make chocolate pudding. It was a sure way to make Papa smile. Chocolate pudding was a treat that they only got once or twice a month. Mama had been the only one who made it, for she said that she didn't have a girl who wouldn't scorch it. Sugar was too expensive, and so was chocolate, to chance a waste. They hadn't had pudding since Mama died. Papa use to always smile and praise Mama's chocolate pudding.

She didn't know how to make pudding, and she didn't figure it was the right time to ask Wanda to teach her. She'd better find the cookbook. She crawled on top the table portion of the big wooden kitchen cabinet and pulled herself up to examine the top shelves. Smells of dried spices, dusty flour, and the rank lard that clung to the outside of the bucket greeted her.

She found the cookbook that one of the East Mattie women had given to Mama. Her church had tried to sell them, but no one bought any. Mama said that in hard times no one needed a cookbook to call for things that no one had in the first place. There sure were lots of recipes.

Clark Gable purred and rubbed himself against her foot that touched the floor as she perched on the cabinet edge and read. She took time to scratch between his ears. Since she'd gotten too big to talk to dolls, she really appreciated having Clark Gable around in hours of need. Anyway, she never had had many dolls in her life, for she only got one every other Christmas, and it never lasted out the two years.

"Be patient, Clark. Soon as I can figure out this recipe, I'll get the pudding made. The leavings in the pan will be all yours to lick. Don't that sound delicious?"

She said no more out loud for it occurred to her that Wanda and Darnella might think she was enjoying herself. Maybe she'd best make a little mad racket! She couldn't let them get in the habit of asking her to make pudding every time they needed her to leave the room.

14

She needed facts more than chocolate pudding, no matter how good it tasted.

She pushed the heavy bean pot loudly to the back of the great cast-iron range, jerked open a stove lid with the lifter, and shoved in lots of wood on top of the kindling Darnella had left there for the next fire. She could read the directions while the stove lids got hot and ready for cooking.

She read aloud to Clark Gable, "'. . . must be cooked slowly over low heat or in a double boiler.' I'm sorry to have to tell you this, Clark, but I got trouble. My fire's so hot it won't be low heat for a good hour, and I don't know what a double boiler is. It says here, 'Take a double boiler, put chocolate in the top, and set in the bottom'!"

Clark Gable meowed loudly, and she didn't blame him. It did sound funny. Better ask Wanda.

As she entered the living room again, Darnella was shouting, "No! No! I won't. I don't care if I do have to leave. No, Wanda, I don't care! I don't care! I don't care."

Girlie had not heard that much yelling out of Darnella in all her life. She just stood there holding the cookbook until Wanda asked, "What do you want, Girlie?"

But Darnella gave her no time to answer. She said, "I wrote down the melon orders just like he told me, and when Galen and Papa came back, Papa starts saying that I can't read, can't write and. . . ." Darnella looked at Girlie, "and lots more. And all in front of Galen as if I was the lowest of. . . ."

Girlie held her finger on the spot where the directions made no sense and got into the conversation. "What'd you say back to Papa, Darnella?"

"I said, 'I'm sorry,' just like my Mama, I said I'm sorry

to that dirty. . . . He fired Galen. Galen's leaving, and I'm leaving with him!"

Quickly Wanda put her hand over Darnella's mouth and said, "Girlie, you want something? You need help with the cookbook?"

There wasn't any use hoping to hear more with Wanda so set about it, so Girlie said, "Yeah, what's a double boiler? It says here for me to put some chocolate in the top half and then for me to set in the bottom. Ain't that weird?"

Wanda stood right in front of Darnella now and talked real cheerful to Girlie, "Oh, don't be a silly. You know what it means. It means to use two pans that fit inside of each other. You're to put chocolate in the top pan and water in the bottom, then set the top pan in the bottom pan. Just like it says. So get on and finish it. And stop trying to hear me and Darnella. We're done talking anyway, ain't we, Darnella?"

Darnella said, "Sure, sure, Wanda," and started upstairs.

The pudding glugged away forever as the air bubbles rose to the top. It cooked slow, being so far from the heat when using double pans. Papa came in from work while it was still cooking. Susy was napping in the doorway between the kitchen and dining room, and Clark Gable had curled up near her for a cat nap. Girlie hoped Papa didn't wake them.

She heard his heavy footsteps coming in the back door to the porch. He wore heavy high-top shoes laced with rawhide, darkened and twisted from thousands of lacings and unlacings. He'd worn the same shoes as long as she could remember, getting them resoled as the need arose. Now he was washing. She could hear the tin dipper clank against the water bucket and the scratch of the wash pan across the enameled service table.

Soon as his cleaning up was finished she'd wave the chocolate pudding in front of the kitchen door. The delicious smell of it would bring him from the porch through that doorway smiling. Mama had often said, "The way to a man's heart is through his stomach," and had at times added, "Thank God, there is some way."

The noise stopped and she held up the pan invitingly. Papa came in. His massive shoulders were curved narrow now and rounded into gloom. His shirt was clinging sweaty to his skin, and Girlie couldn't tell where water drippings from his face and hair ended and the sweat started. His light brown hair was graying near the edges and thinning on top. Wrinkles creased around his pale blue eyes, which were squinting against the water. He wasn't smiling.

Nor did Papa smile during the supper, nor once say just how fine the pudding had turned out. So no one else talked much either, not even when dishes were being washed and wiped and the yard chores attended to. But after they had all gone to bed, Girlie was awakened to some loud whispering. Nita wasn't in bed with her. She got up and, lowering her head not to hit the low spot in the ceiling, crept into the other bedroom. There sat Darnella, Nita, and Wanda in a huddle on the bed amidst the quilts Mama had made.

Nita was saying, "If Darnella leaves, then I ain't staying either. I was to get to ride Old Bell to high school. Mama promised and Papa said 'no' just like that." Nita snapped her fingers. "Said Old Bell's a western horse and would never make it across the bridges. I could break him of that habit of balking at bridges. I know I could."

17

Wanda shushed Nita, "There, there, things will get all worked out. Now you go get back in bed, okay?"

Girlie scurried to beat it to bed herself before Nita caught her listening.

Next morning she was awakened by Nita shouting at someone. It was Susy.

"No, no, no! Wanda, come get your kid. She's poking dried rose petals down the tea kettle spout. She'll fall on her face on a hot stove doing things like that."

By the time Girlie got downstairs, Nita was slapping Susy's hands and saying, "Bad girl! Bad girl!"

Girlie agreed with her, "Bad girl, Susy. Them's my rose petals for my underwear drawer." She squeezed Susy's fingers to make her let go the petals.

Suddenly Darnella was there too, trying to make Girlie let go of Susy's hand, and Wanda was grabbing for Susy.

Wanda crooned, "There, there baby. It's all right. You're not a bad girl. You're Mommy's little lady."

In the midst of it all Girlie looked up to see Papa. He was just standing to one side, ready to go to the fields. He was frowning. How many times before had he caught his wife and his daughters in one big free-for-all and had laughed his head off at the show? "Women are more fun than a bunch of bear-cats," he'd say. This time he left without a word.

It was Nita who began to laugh. She pushed back away from Wanda, grabbed for the kitchen cabinet for support. Her hand landed in the small dishpan where one of Darnella's dresses was soaking. Off slipped the pan of sudsy water and down with it went Nita. She sat there laughing. "Who told you to leave a dress soaking on the kitchen cabinet, Darnella? Do I look like Mommy's little lady?"

"I . . . I'm sorry, I was . . . you look so funny, Nita."
Darnella joined in the laughter.

Wanda must have thought that they were poking fun,
for she said, "It's not funny!" But as Nita spread the suds
all about her, Wanda's voice lost its sting, and she
laughed too.

They all laughed until Nita's laughter came out in
bursts that soon sounded very much like sobs. Girlie
quickly took Susy from Wanda's arms and let Wanda
draw Nita near to her bosom and cuddle her and coo,
"Nita, honey. Stop crying. You're coming home with me.
There's a high school just three blocks from our house,
and you don't need to ride no balky horse to get there. It's
all right. I'll take care of you. Now get quiet, there's
something I've got to tell you and Girlie."

Girlie asked, "Is it about the whispering?"

Wanda spoke soberly, "I'll tell you clear and simple.
Darnella has let her mad against Papa drive her into the
arms of a man, and now she's obliged to stay there. She'll
be marrying Galen tomorrow."

So, that was what had been settled in the middle of the
night. Girlie couldn't believe it. Galen had worked for
Papa all summer. Papa always hired men he didn't care
much for, maybe because he hated the fact that he had
to hire help at times tending his melons and peanuts.
Papa himself had to hire out to other farmers in other
states during slack season to make ends meet. He hated
being a hired man; he hated having to hire others to help
him out. And now Papa was allowing Darnella to marry
a hired man. Or was he? "Does Papa know about it?"
Girlie asked.

"S-h-h-h," Wanda whispered. "Papa knows."

19

Nita asked, "And does Papa know that I'm going with you?"

"Papa knows."

When, Girlie wondered, did Papa find out all these things? It had to come from the whispers in the night. She never heard them discussed aloud. Some things never got spoken at all, even in whispers.

"What about me? Will I have to keep house for Papa all by myself?"

Wanda touched her arm, "Papa said he'd take care of you."

Girlie relaxed. Papa wanted her. He needed her. She'd manage somehow to please him.

Almost a week went by, and Girlie didn't upset Papa by nagging or asking questions. She just waited. It was a long quiet wait. The first of the week Darnella had packed her pillowcase full of her clothes and took the pillow plus two new quilts out of Mama's trunk and the feather ticking off of Mama and Papa's bed.

Papa said, "I slept on straw ticking all my life until I married your Mama. Won't matter none to start again."

Galen had waited out front by the scrub oak while Darnella carried the things all out, and then they left. They were probably married by now. Girlie wondered where they found a house.

Nita never fought, nor acted prissy. Even little Susy was quiet and stayed out of meanness. Everyone waited to see what Papa had planned.

Maybe Papa would break his rules about girls not helping out in the fields on a regular basis. He had to get another hired man right away or have girl-help soon enough. Now if Papa did settle on having her help in the field, cleaning out the last of the melons, then maybe he'd settle on her pulling peanuts too. And then maybe he'd plant some cotton next year, and he could stay home the year around and farm and not have to go off picking peas up North every June. Because he'd not be able to go away anymore, now that she was the only one left at home and would have no one to stay with. Mama always said it wouldn't hurt Papa any to swallow his pride, and she was exactly right. She'd tell him that soon as Wanda left with Nita.

Wanda came in like a mind reader and said, "Nita, start gathering your things together and, Girlie, you better get your things together right now too."

"But I ain't going with you, Wanda. I got to stay with Papa."

Wanda's eyes had been crying. She said, "Papa says you're to pack."

Girlie stared at her. Not once had she considered the thought that she'd be going along with Nita. She'd just been sure that Papa wanted her to stay, needed her. Besides, Wanda couldn't take in more than one extra kid. In the city you have to pay cash for most all your needs. Nita was the one that needed high school right now. And maybe she'd like a city school. Her sister Lil, who was the reader in the family, said there was no schools like city schools. They had big buildings and libraries and all kinds of classes, and sometimes you even got to choose what class you wanted to take. You could even learn things like algebra if you had a mind to. "If Papa says I got to go with you, then I got to go."

Wanda was silent for a bit. Then she reached into her apron pocket and held out an old ledger. "Girlie, I found this among some of Mama's things. It's old, and Papa has long forgotten it. You take it to do your figuring on. I wish you was going with me too, Girlie, honest I do, but Papa's taking you to another place. I better leave it to him to tell."

Wanda walked away, and Girlie stood looking at the ledger. She did need paper. But she needed it for something more than figuring. Facts were flitting in and out of her mind, not staying, for they formed no shape to give them meaning. She needed to write them down, to hold them until more came by to be added to the list. One day the shape would be there in the list, making sense. She was sure of it. Mama always said, "Calm down and let's gather the facts together, and then we'll decide." Okay, she'd start gathering and listing what she gathered.

She put the ledger carefully in her empty pillowcase, and then put in her three dresses neatly folded. The everyday home dress was made of flour sacking, but it looked nice. Mama made her own patterns, and she had had a way with making dresses that were becoming and stylish. Her school dress was made of sugar sacking, a sack of finer quality, but Mama had made the Sunday dress of store-bought material: dotted swiss. Nita, who had light hair like Papa and the other girls, had one in blue. Girlie's was yellow to set off her black hair and eyes and brown skin. Each had a large satin sash with tiny flowers embroidered by Mama on the section across the front. They wore them to her funeral, since Mama had always liked her girls dressed nice in public.

That took care of all her belongings except for Clark Gable. She rounded him up. She wasn't about to go anywhere without him.

Not a word was said as they packed, until finally Nita asked out loud what Girlie wouldn't let herself ask. "Do you think Papa will take you over to Molly's?"

22

Molly was the oldest sister, and it stood to reason. She and her husband Malford (he liked people to call them Mol and Mal but no one did) were not doing bad as farmers. Not that they had as much money as Wanda who lived in St. Louis, or Rose who lived in Poplar Bluff, but they got by.

"You'll have some fun living with Russel!" Nita said.

Nita knew how to force a body to think on things she'd as soon forget. Russel was Molly's son. He was also a spoiled brat, and Girlie hated him. She was so full of hate that she couldn't even snap back at Nita's smart statement about enjoying Russel's company. She would die rather than live in the same house with that bratty kid, and let him torment her and Clark Gable. Papa wouldn't do that to her. Or would he? Russel was the first grandson and the apple of Papa's eye. At least that's what Molly told anyone in the world that would listen. What was worse, Russel even looked like Papa—a little fat Papa, as puffy as a roasted marshmallow on two toothpicks. It made Girlie boil just to think about him. She grabbed Clark Gable and went outside to wait in a place where she could think and talk.

"Clark, don't you worry. If Papa does plan to leave us over at Molly's, it's probably just for a short spell. He talked a lot last year about how nice it'd be to take the last load of melons into St. Louis and sell them. That's surely what he plans to do. Just leave us with Molly until he makes the trip."

Papa called to break her thoughts, "Girlie, get on the wagon with the others."

They drove only a half mile to the railroad, and all sat in the wagon until the freight train was spotted. Then Papa got out and flagged it down. Wanda and Susy and

Nita got into the caboose and waved good-bye. They were crying. So was Girlie. She kept on crying and crying, even after she and Papa got back into the wagon.

"Now, stop it, Girlie. They ain't dead. They'll be coming to visit at Christmas or at least by next summer."

It wasn't just Nita and Wanda she was crying about. Couldn't Papa tell that? Why didn't he tell her what he had decided? Why wouldn't he give her the right to not go to Molly's and live with that pain, Russel? Russel had once tied two empty pork and bean cans on Clark Gable's tail. She bawled even louder at the thought, and held Clark so tight that he nearly clawed her.

Papa cracked the whip on the horses, and they went galloping right on toward Molly's, down Black River Road and a sharp swing up and over Black River bridge. It caught Girlie so off guard that she hardly had time to drop her hold on Clark and clutch her hand tightly over her nose. She always held her nose when crossing bridges because, if they should go off the bridge by chance, she didn't know how to swim. But they didn't need to *cross* Black River to get to Molly's! Then Papa took another quick turn to the right, and Girlie knew where they were going. She took her hand from her nose and began talking soft and sweetly to Clark. "Everything's all right. It's all right." And it was, for they were heading for Lil's.

She hadn't thought of Lil, for Lil was the worst off of any of the girls. Once she had done without food for three days, until her husband Symond finally went and asked Molly and Malford for a handout. Molly lived almost directly across the river, which meant Girlie would go to the same school as Russel.

Lil had a seven-year-old son, Bobby, but he didn't go to school. He wasn't real bright, and couldn't learn like most

24

kids do. Papa never mentioned the fact that Lil too had born a boy. Papa more or less ignored things that weren't perfect. He sure ought to ignore Russel, but he didn't.

Bobby was standing in the way as Papa pulled into Lil's front yard. Papa pulled the horses to a stop. "Whoa! Lil! Lil! Will you come move your child!"

Lil came running out of the house and quickly sent Bobby skirting around to the backyard away from the horses. "Well, Papa, Girlie, I never expected to see you in the middle of the week. Something wrong?"

Papa stayed seated, holding the reins. He cleared his throat and said, "Lil, I'm giving you Girlie. She's got good sense, and she can cook fair enough. She's yours to keep. Get down, Girlie."

"But, Papa. . . ." Lil stood there with a strange look and then nodded her head, and Girlie thought it was all right to get down. She took her pillowcase and Clark Gable, and jumped to the ground.

"Don't worry, Papa, I'll see you even before Christmas. I won't be so far away as Nita."

But Papa wasn't worrying. He just hit the reins hard and turned the wagon around and went off down the road.

Girlie stood staring after him. She must be imagining things. She knew that Papa wasn't talking lightly, but he couldn't be giving her to Lil for good. He just needed time to get things all straightened out in his mind.

She'd better start getting facts down in her ledger, before her imagination got her believing crazy things.

three

THE fact was that she stood in Lil's front yard, her belongings at her feet, Clark Gable in one arm, and her good dress held high in her other hand. And another fact was that Papa indeed had buried Mama way up on Sand Hill. But the second fact didn't help her understand the first fact one bit. She'd need a lot more facts before the shape would come clear to her.

"Lil, what does Papa mean? Why can't I stay in my own house with him? Why is Papa acting like this?"

"Sh-sh, honey, it's all right. You're here with me, and that's all you need worry about now. Give him time. Give him time."

Suddenly Bobby was there beside her, peeking inside her pillowcase. "This yours, Girlie? Is this yours, Girlie?" He was pulling out all her clothes.

Lil caught his hands and held them and whispered softly, "No, Bobby. You can't have Girlie's belongings."

"Bobby ain't hurting anything. Here, I'll hold my Sunday dress, and he can't hurt the others."

Again Lil whispered, "These things are Girlie's, Bobby. You have a new sister, now."

"I'm *Aunt* Girlie. I'm not Bobby's sister. Why are you whispering, Lil?"

Lil shooed Bobby to the backyard again. "Go finish your toad house, honey. Here, take Girlie's cat with you. He'd like to see your nice toad house. Now, Girlie, let's go find a place for your stuff. I always start out whispering when I have to scold Bobby. That way if he don't mind me and I have to get mad at him the most, I might end up yelling. If I started out yelling then I'd have to end up doing something stronger like hitting, and I don't see no sense in having to do that."

Lil had a way, be it a strange way, of controlling *her* temper. At least when Lil did something strange, she was quick to make sense of it. Girlie followed Lil into the house and watched while she laid her dresses up on a little shelf between the chimney supports in the bedroom.

"You'll be sleeping on the cot in the front room, but you can come here and use the bedroom to dress after Symond gets up and out in the morning."

There was only one bedroom in Lil's little house, and it held their bed and Bobby's big crib. Then there was the front room and the kitchen, and that was all except for a small back porch. But it was a nice house. Not real clean like Wanda liked things, but clean enough, sort of like the way Mama used to keep things, easy to live with.

And Lil's house was filled with the wonderful smell of yeast dough! Lil had no money to buy yeast, but she'd gotten a start from Molly once and been growing her own yeast ever since for free. It gave the house a good smell, and Girlie wouldn't mind at all coming here for a *visit*.

"Girlie, come help me fix supper. Black River School already started two days ago, because they let out in September for cotton picking vacation. You'll be starting school in the morning and that means we got planning to do, and things to settle before Symond gets in for supper."

Starting school was not what a visitor did. She was really here to stay.

"Symond is sure going to be surprised, ain't he?"

Lil handed her some dry beans to sort over and wash clean. "He'll be right surprised, but it'll be all right. We'll manage. We always have. One way or another."

And it was all right with Symond. He was a good-natured man. He didn't act real surprised; just said in his slow easy talk, "Well, Girlie, I hope you can put up with this little rascal of ours." Bobby was climbing all over Symond while he talked. "And I hope you like that teacher over at Black River School. They tell me he's a corker. Seems he rattles a few heads every day of the week over there."

Symond hadn't meant any harm by his remarks, but they sure left Girlie scared. That night she dreamed she was in her own school doing eighth-grade work, and being praised. And when she came home at night there was Mama and Papa. But then she woke up in Lil's house with Lil telling her to borrow a sheet of paper from Russel for the first day. Symond would manage some way to get her a tablet by tomorrow.

Black River School was a one-room school. There were sixty-two pupils enrolled, and only nine of them not related in some way by marriage or something. Even Girlie was Russel's aunt, though most everyone thought they were cousins because they were the same age. Girlie was in eighth grade and had her promotion card to prove it, but Russel was just in seventh. Right off he started making a fuss about that. Some help he was for a girl scared to death on her first day at a new school.

"Mr. Cory, Girlie and me was always in the same grade before I moved, and she can't be in the eighth grade now."

Mr. Cory was a short man, a fat-in-the-middle man, and a man who made a statement once and that was all. "I've never tolerated family feuds in my school, for if I did I'd hear not one word of book recitation. I've taught this school full of mean kinfolk for ten years without one ounce of trouble. Sit down Russel, and shut up. I'm going by her promotion card, and that's that."

Mr. Cory went over and sat down by the huge furnace that sat in one corner of the large classroom. His chair was the big wooden kind that all teachers have, that tilts. He tilted way back and laughed. "Can you imagine me having to listen to the East Matties and the West Matties airing their family problems?"

Everyone in the class roared, and Girlie had to smile. The East Matties were the strongest bunch of Christians in the whole country, and the West Matties were the strongest bunch of dirty drunks known to anyone. Even Girlie knew that. No one bothered to hide that fact through whispers.

Mr. Cory stopped laughing. "Yahoo—sixth graders, you'll come up front first today. Rest of you that can read, see your assignments on the blackboard. Trudy, get them first graders reciting to you."

Girlie started to read the column of assignments for the eighth graders. She wasn't halfway to the bottom when she saw it. On the second board under the heading,

STARRED PROBLEMS MUST BE COMPLETED BY ALL
SEVENTH AND EIGHTH GRADERS BEFORE COTTON
PICKING VACATION OR BE FLUNKED. ANY HELP FROM
YOUR PARENTS = FLUNKED.

The first one said: A man has a duck, a fox, and some corn and must take them all across the river safely to the other side. He can only take one thing in his boat on each crossing. Remember the duck will eat the corn if left together, and the fox will eat the duck if left together. Tell how the man got them all safely to the other side.

What great fun! She had never realized that a quiz like this could be called school work. She quickly wrote out the answer and started in on the next problem of arranging a group of nickels, when she realized Mr. Cory was standing above her head reading her paper.

"Good girl, Girlie Webster. You'll do all right in this school. I like to see a new student dig right into their lesson assignments."

She liked Mr. Cory. He wasn't a bad corker; he was a good corker. Wait until she told Symond and Lil the truth of the matter about what a fine teacher Mr. Cory was. No teacher who gave problems like that as assignments could be all bad! She went on to work every last one of the starred problems.

"Eighth graders, bring your geography papers and come to the front."

Seven of the biggest boys and girls got up from their desks and headed to the front of the room. Girlie looked again at the eighth-grade assignments. Geography: Do questions 1 through 10, page 3. Due time: 9:45. She couldn't move.

"Girlie Webster, you better pay attention when I talk. I'll say it twice *this* time since you're new. Eighth graders bring your geography papers and come to the front, that means right up here."

"I didn't do my geography," she whispered.

Quickly Mr. Cory moved between the rows of desks. "What? Can't you read? Your geography paper is due right now, nine forty-five." WHAM! His huge hand slapped her across the face shaking her head with such impact that she couldn't help but scream. He remained beside her, and she dared not look up at him. He had the problems she had just solved in his hand. "Fine, fine work. Looks like you got some talent here. I'll take these right now so no one copies. Come, sit up front with your class, and you get this work made up tonight besides your regular homework assignment. Get up."

Her face hurt, and she heard Russel's snicker all the way from the back of the room. But she couldn't let those things keep her from the fact that Mr. Cory had said she had a talent.

Girlie thought now that she knew what kind of corker Mr. Cory was, and by the end of the day she was sure that she knew. At noontime, five boys got in a fight way out in back of the baseball diamond. Mr. Cory cut five thick willow branches and peeled them while everyone watched, then gave each boy one. He made them circle the big old school furnace in the corner and start whipping each other. Said if anyone didn't do a good job on another, he'd take care of that one personally. It was an awful sight to behold no matter who would be the beholder. Girlie turned her back.

At two o'clock when it came time for the first graders to repeat what Trudy, the biggest girl in the room, had

31

been practicing them to recite, one little West Mattie boy didn't talk. His older brother explained that he understood everything but he couldn't talk. Mr. Cory built a small fire under his chair by lighting a match to the wadded-up sheets of paper.

The West Mattie boy screamed, "Father! Mother!" These were the words that Trudy had been practicing them on.

After school, she got out her ledger and recorded the fact she had surmised about Mr. Cory:

"Good and bad can be in the same person."

Lil saw her writing and said, "What's that you're writing on? Oh, you don't have to use that old ledger, honey. Symond cleaned one of the West Mattie's chicken house, the one that runs the store, and got you a tablet, two pencils, and a new ruler too. That ought to last you until cotton picking vacation."

The tablet did last for the two months until cotton picking vacation started. Girlie was saving. She always wrote on both sides and clear out to the edges of her paper. And even if it meant walking four miles to and from, she hoped to hire out to Molly and Malford and pick cotton and buy her own tablets from then on.

All the talk at school now was about getting their starred problems before closing so Mr. Cory wouldn't flunk them. Girlie didn't have to worry for Mr. Cory had hers, but she did have to be careful not to help anyone else. She shuddered to think what Mr. Cory would do to her in that case. Russel hadn't even started on his problems, and that meant trouble for him for sure. But that was his business, not hers. Then, one day, when it was Girlie's turn to stay in at recess to clean the blackboards,

Russel stayed in to help her. Right off, she was sure of his reason for doing it.

"Girlie, you tell me answers to them problems, and I'll wash the board for you."

"I can wash it myself. I like washing blackboards."

"Girlie, you tell me them answers or I'll goose you in front of the boys."

"You just try it, Russel, and you'll wish you hadn't. There is no way you can make me help you. I'd die first."

Russel dusted some chalk from his hands and said, "Well, we'll see about that. Remember, I tried to be nice about it first." He left her alone, and that was all she heard of it for a few days.

Then, the weekend just before cotton picking vacation, Molly and Malford and Russel came for a visit at Lil's. She knew it had to do with Russel and the starred problems, but neither Molly nor Malford let on about that at first. They acted like they were just coming for a nice visit with Lil and Symond.

They drove up about ten o'clock Saturday morning, catching everybody busy. Lil was cutting out a blouse pattern for Girlie by fitting her with pieces of an old *St. Louis Post-Dispatch* newspaper that Mr. Cory had let her bring home from school. Lil had traded some raised doughnuts to one of the widowed West Mattie men for a red satin slip that had belonged to his wife. It was to be a fine blouse to wear for graduation. That was seven months off, but Lil was a lot like Mama for planning ahead and managing. Girlie read to Bobby while she was being fitted, and Bobby sat watching his reflection in the side of an aluminum tea pot, making his face change to funny shapes by moving his head.

They were all laughing at Bobby, even Symond who'd

taken on the job of kneading the weekly supply of light-bread. It was an extra big batch, for Symond had heard that Papa wasn't eating right and was losing weight. He had a job over that way and could take some bread to him.

"What you all laughing about?" asked Malford from the doorway. "Don't you even hear company when it comes? What you doing there, Symond?"

Symond hung his head a bit. "I'm giving Lil a hand with the light-bread."

Malford yelled back outside, "Come on in, they're home. We caught them at the right time. Just in time for light-bread. Come take a look at Symond in an apron. He's got that kitchen table fairly dancing. Well, keep it going, Sy. The bread should go real good with this mess of grinnel that me and Russel caught."

"Mostly me!" Russel said as he held up a string filled with the long greenish fish.

Lil said, "They're fine looking fish and we sure accept them, if you'll throw in the guarantee that Molly will help me cook them. No one has a way with grinnel like Molly; hers are never one bit mushy."

Molly moved in fast with a pleased look on her face. She was little and spritely. When she married Malford, folks said it proved that opposites attract.

"It's in the deal, Lil. Now give me them fish, and Russel you go on out and play with Bobby. I tell you that boy's so mean I can't do a thing with him." Molly said it lovingly.

Lil carefully folded up the newspaper pattern, making her room welcome for company. Girlie hated to see Lil so flattered by this visit when she knew sooner or later Malford and Molly would be trying to force her to do Russel's starred problems. Well, she wasn't going to do them.

Molly had already begun cleaning the fish. "It's true. I guess that I do cook grinnel good. Most everyone lacks the skill of doing it just right, even Mama, though Lord knows she taught me plenty of other things. First I make them bring the fish back to me alive, and I split their tails and let them bleed to death properly. I did that right off when Russel got in with these. See, I made the split right here. You look too, Girlie, I've a feeling you're going to have a talent for cooking. Well, when they are bled right and fried fast and brown, they're the best eating fish there is, in my opinion. Where's your flour and cornmeal, Lil? And, Girlie, go dig me a half-gallon jar of kraut out of the fruit cellar. I like fried kraut with just a smidge of sugar in it when I fry fish."

Girlie ran outside to get the kraut but continued running right on past the cellar, for she heard the horrible growling noises Clark Gable made when being attacked. Russel was holding Clark down with his knee, while he finished tying the last paper bag on the cat's feet. She ran to rescue Clark but, before she could, Russel tossed him out and roared with laughter when poor Clark couldn't walk. She managed to slug Russel before leaping to free the cat. Russel had tied hard knots in the strings that held the bags, and she had to use her knife to cut them.

"Russel, you ever get close to my cat again and I'll . . . I'll. . . ."

"You'll, what? You can't lick me and you know it."

He might be right about that, and then again he might not be. As mad as she was right now she figured she could at least make him sorry for tangling with her.

"Russel, you're going to flunk, because I sure ain't going to help you. I don't care if you did bring Molly over to ask me."

35

Russel stood his distance as if he wasn't so sure he could lick her, but he still talked back. "Girlie, you ain't got no place to run. I heard Grandpaw gave you away. I don't blame him. And I don't blame him for never tacking a name on you. You ain't worth it."

That did it. She dropped Clark Gable and screaming for the whole world to hear, "Put 'em up, Russel," she lit in to him. Sure Papa was disappointed when she came out a girl. She was the tenth, and it was a fact that Papa told Dr. Lester that he didn't have no more girl names left in him. And it was a fact that Dr. Lester had put Girl Baby on her birth certificate and everyone had called her Girlie ever since, but Russel better hold that tongue of his. She grabbed hold of his brown hair with one hand and hit him in his soft fat belly with the other. He was hitting her something furious too, but she didn't care.

"Girlie, Girlie, stop it!" Lil was shouting.

"Separate them! Separate them." Malford was yelling the orders and carrying them out himself.

Lil held Girlie, so she couldn't move while she caught her breath.

Molly was wiping Russel's forehead. "Girlie, if you don't learn to control that temper of yours, I don't know what in this world is going to happen to you."

"Russel tied paper bags on Clark Gable's feet!"

Malford said, "You got to learn that boys will be boys. All young boys tease cats. There ain't no harm done. Russel ain't hurt, he can handle himself, but you do got to control that bad temper."

Lil said, "Girlie, better get the kraut. What's done is done."

She obeyed Lil. She figured Russel was hurting some

anyway, even if he didn't dare let on. By the time she got back to the kitchen with the kraut, things had settled down. Symond had put the bread dough to rest, and he and Malford had taken chairs in the front room and were swapping stories about Darnella's man, Galen.

Malford was saying, "He's about as low as a snake's belly in a wagon rut."

Both the man talk and the woman talk was interesting, and Girlie wanted to divide her time between the two. She heard Molly say, "Lil, remember when we helped Mama make that big batch of kraut the year you met Symond?"

If the talk was to be of Mama, then she better listen to the women for some new facts to put in her ledger.

Lil smiled. "I'm not about to ever forget that time. Symond kept hanging around to eat cabbage cores. Claimed he loved cabbage cores. Told me later that he about died that night from eating so many. Now if that ain't love, what is?"

Girlie stepped in right between Molly and Lil and started jostling the peeled potatoes around in their water to get them clean. "Lil, if Symond had died from eating all them cabbage cores and got buried in his family plot, would you have wanted to be buried by him or in Papa's family plot by your Grandma and Grandpa Webster?"

Both Lil and Molly stopped peeling potatoes at once, and then Molly let out a loud laugh and said, "Girlie, if you don't come up with some good ones."

Lil didn't laugh, but she did take great effort to control her words. "Girlie, it don't make no difference where a body is buried. No difference at all. If two people love each other, that's all that matters a whit."

Molly said, "Hey, Girlie, let me help you finish setting that table while Lil slices them potatoes. Too many cooks spoils the broth."

Molly placed the rest of the plates around on the small kitchen table and had to add a couple of tin pie pans to have enough for all. In the center of the table was Lil's inheritance from Mama—a blue cut-glass pitcher, casting blue diamond pictures on the wall, making blue speckles on Molly's apron.

Molly said, "Girlie, run out to the car and bring me in some pickles and Bermuda onions. Lil, I ain't so sure I like the idea you making yeast rolls. Now Malford is going to be expecting me to try your tricks, and I ain't got no luck that way. I guess I take after Papa's side on light-bread. Girlie, call in the menfolks too. It'll be ready by the time they wash up. And wash Bobby. My gosh, it'll take a corn cob and lye soap to get the rust off that boy."

Things stayed so pleasant, you could cut the honey words with a warm knife. Even Russel sat there nodding his head yes and no at the right times, and causing no trouble. Girlie took advantage of the peace to enjoy the good eating. The only meat she'd had for the six weeks she'd been at Lil's had been an occasional piece of hog fat rolled in cornmeal that Symond's folks had let them have. Mostly they lived on Lil's wonderful light-bread and wild greens such as narrow dock, slick dock, lambs quarter, and lay flat, and speckled dick. There weren't even many wild berries within walking distance, not like over at Papa's, where Girlie used to pick buckets of berries for the jelly and pies that he loved.

She wondered what he was eating now. He wouldn't have time to go picking berries or greens. And how was he managing the farm all alone? Had he gotten all the melons sold; did he take them to St. Louis; did he get a hired man to help out with the peanuts? She asked, "Anyone hear how Papa's managing?"

They heard her question, she was sure, but no one answered. Molly said, "Lil, you don't mind if I just make a meal out of your light-bread, do you? I tell you I cuss that doctor over Qulin, every time I eat, for pulling out all my teeth saying they was poisoning my body. I felt *worse* afterward. I'm likely to die now of starvation, for I just can't get these false ones to fit so I can chew good."

Everyone laughed except Girlie who wanted to point out that Molly's teeth could drive others crazy with their clicking. But she held her tongue and finished her fish.

Malford said, "It ain't because she don't try to make them fit. She's got my grinding wheel out everyday or so grinding them down a little here or there. They got a money-back guarantee that they won't break, but I'm wondering if that guarantee holds good if she grinds them clean away."

Everyone laughed again, so Malford kept his place as the talker of the moment. "Symond, life sure ain't treating you too bad, eating light-bread and all this under a big shiny electric light bulb."

Bobby had reached up and turned on the light. Lil quickly turned it off again and said apologetically, "Symond made a deal with one of the East Mattie men who runs the light company office. He gets our monthly rate all paid by doing his chores. I don't know yet how we're going to manage this month though. The rate's 71¢, and for some reason we went over. I just got the bill. It's 74¢, and me without a penny. I just hope they don't turn off the electricity."

"If they do," Molly got a smart look on her face, "you

can do like the rest of us *poor* people and burn coal oil lamps."

Girlie was feeling terrible. It had all been her fault. One of the East Mattie women, a sister to the light company Mattie, was a schoolteacher over at Poplar Bluff. Each weekend she rode the bus home, and she brought them library books. Girlie had overdone it. Read too many times to Bobby by electric light.

Malford reached in his pocket and pulled out a nickel and flipped it on the table. "Mol, don't ride 'em. You know Symond makes his living by swapping. Ain't his fault that one of his swaps gets him an electric light and we don't. Now that nickel's yourn, and you keep the change, hear me?"

Russel said, "I made a nickel myself riding the horse for the sorghum press, and would of still made more except that West Mattie bunch wore me out until I was all hunkered over and fell off and got cussed out, and I quit."

Symond reached out and took the money. "You sure this is all right now? Honest Injun?"

"Sure, I'm sure. Great balls of cat hair, you think I'd throw it down there on the table if I didn't mean for you to take it?"

Girlie hated that expression. She reached down and touched Clark Gable, who was sitting quietly under her chair. He purred softly.

Malford pushed his chair into the front room. "Lil, now you better turn your electric light on. It's clouding over. Reminds me of the time Russel was born. Boy, the wind was roaring right through the naked trees. It was the middle of January. I can hear the moan of that wind now as it came down the chimney, and Molly said that doctor better get here fast. Your Mama couldn't come help out, for she was sick unto death with carrying Girlie. She was not due for three months. Now that's when we was glad we'd put our money in a telephone, instead of electric lights like some people, though be it, a telephone is a sight cheaper. Well, that wind was making a hateful racket banging brittle brush against the icy dirt of the ditch dumps. I held up our coal oil lantern to see if it was the Doc's car I heard. It was. He had this Sixteen model brass-radiator Ford and. . . ."

Girlie left the room. She'd heard this story a hundred times before. There wouldn't be anything new said in it. It was all about the great night that Molly broke the continuous chain of girls in the Webster family by bringing mighty Russel into the world.

She took out her ledger and recorded a very old fact about Mama:

When Russel was born, I had three months to go, and Mama was very very sick.

She got back into the front room in time to hear Malford say, "And the Doc says, 'What you going to name your baby?' And I says, 'I don't have a thing to do with the matter. It's been settled for thirty some odd years. His Grandpaw has named him Russel!' "

Russel laughed. "Boy, Grandpaw give me something he didn't give you, didn't he, Girlie?"

Symond jumped up from his chair and announced loudly, "It sure is about to storm. It surely is. I'll bet you it'll be pouring buckets within just a few short minutes."

Girlie appreciated Symond changing the subject, but it wasn't working. Neither Molly nor Malford made a move to leave. They'd never stayed two seconds after spotting a storm when they came visiting Mama, even when she was bad sick. But now they stayed. Malford went into a new stage of the story. "By then it was lighting up toward daytime and the stars was fading out, and. . . ."

Symond walked about impatiently. "Malford, we're going to have to grease that throat of yours to cut down on the racket you're making. I wasn't a joking. It's coming up a real humdinger of a storm. Is there anything we can do to help you?"

Malford leaned back until his kitchen chair touched the wall. "Well, now that you mention it, I think Girlie might give us a hand on something. Now I never was much on figures, and Russel here takes after me, and I'm proud, but this Mr. Cory has notions in his head that everyone ought to be . . . well, you know, everyone ought to see right into them crazy problems he assigns. I ain't calling them arithmetic, for it ain't even rightly that, but a body can't reason let alone argue with Mr. Cory. No question about it, Russel will flunk if he don't turn in that paper. Russel tells me that Mr. Cory says that Girlie here has a talent. I think that was his words, right, Russel?"

"Them are his very words."

Malford continued, "And seeing how we're all kin, I guess it would only be right and proper that we extend a helping hand when another is in need, right, Lil?"

"I been thinking just about that very thing. I been thinking that I might not be out of place to ask if Girlie couldn't possibly come and stay with you folks during cotton picking vacation and get herself some cash money for school clothes. She is a help, she's good help. . . . You see how she's been tending Bobby, and she can fry up breakfast faster than me, and she is your kin Molly . . . !"

42

Molly sat as if in deep thought. Girlie could only think of one thing herself: Why hadn't Lil mentioned this to her? Had she whispered to Symond about it in the night? Didn't she like having her there? Or had Girlie done something wrong? Of course she knew that there was no cash in the house. Lil had almost cried the other day when she saw little Bobby fondle one of the Mattie kid's toy wagon. If she could go to Molly's and earn money, she would buy Bobby a toy wagon with the first dollars she made. She would do that, and then she would buy material for Lil and herself.

Then Lil wouldn't have to give her warnings as she had about the blouse to be made from the red satin slip. "Now don't let others know where this come from. Don't ever tell anyone where you got it. But don't you be ashamed inside yourself about getting it like I did. It was honest; but until people get so they are above belittling and poking fun at others' ways and means, then it's best you not tell and let them do you damage with their talk. We're responsible for what we let other folks know about us. Remember that, Girlie?"

Girlie understood. She could watch Lil scrape the insides of an eggshell clean to get the last bit of food hanging there, as she had this morning. She knew that money could mean a lot to Lil. But she didn't like seeing Lil so quick to trade her off. For a moment she hoped that Papa had had enough time to come to his senses, and would come riding in and say that he was ready now to take her back home. Oh, how she hated to go to Molly's and live in the same house with Russel, but she'd have to do it. For the cash money she would do it. . . . Mr. Cory didn't say that aunts couldn't help, just parents.

"I'll help Russel write his paper," she said.

Russel's grin went from ear to ear. Girlie wanted to bust him one.

Molly said, "Cotton picking vacation lasts for a month and a half, but I guess it is the least I can do. Malford can come by and get Girlie after the paper of Russel's gets wrote and accepted by Mr. Cory. My, that storm's getting close. We better be getting home in a hurry, Malford. Oh . . . there won't be no need for her to bring that cat of hers."

Girlie watched them run like crazy for their car. She had a misery feeling. Bobby would love Clark Gable, and Lil would take good care of him but already she ached with missing him. Her talent that was worth the value of room and board for a month and a half was small comfort. She must keep her mind to the fact that she'd be earning cash money by picking cotton. Also, chances were good she'd get more facts for her ledger, as she'd be around Molly for days on end.

four

THE day before cotton picking vacation, at five minutes
before the bell rang, Girlie handed Russel the paper she
wrote for him and said, "Better get it in your own hand-
writing."

Russel didn't even have time to read it, just as Girlie
had planned. He started writing as fast as an auctioneer
talks. He got it copied seconds before the bell rang, and
Mr. Cory reached out his hand to collect the papers. That
ought to make Russel sweat, in case Mr. Cory quizzed
them on how they got their answers.

The next morning Lil helped Girlie collect her dresses
and put them in her pillowcase. "Leave your red satin
blouse. You'll not need it during cotton picking time. I'll
hang it in a safe spot to keep it nice for special, for your
graduation. We'll take good care of Clark Gable too."

Girlie gave Clark one last big hug. Somewhere in the
back of her mind was the worry that it was her own fault

that she had to leave, because Lil didn't like her or she had done something wrong. And she had a queasy feeling about that right up to the time she heard the *"A-ooo-ga, A-ooo-ga"* of Malford's horn.

She walked to the door and looked out. "Well, come on, Girlie, I'm already late. I had a blowout on the way over, and I told Molly I'd be back short of an hour."

Girlie twisted the end of the pillowcase and, without turning to look at Bobby or Lil, started to go meet Malford. Lil grabbed her back for just a minute, and said, "Molly's better off than we are, Girlie. Be glad about it."

Still she couldn't look. "Good-bye, Bobby. Good-bye, Lil. Good-bye, Clark," and she ran.

In the days that followed, one of the hardest things to get used to was Russel's language. When he wanted to go to the toilet, he just said, "I have to go hocky." Right out loud he said it. She had never said that word out loud in her whole life, and she never would. The least he could do was whisper it. Some things are right to be whispered. She'd never thought about that before. She wrote that fact in her ledger. The first fact to be collected at Molly's. That made six facts in her ledger now, but still no shape to them that made sense.

Picking cotton wasn't entirely new to her. She had done it along with Nita and Darnella for the last two years. Mama had allowed them to hire out to a neighbor. She said every woman needed to know how to do it, in case of emergency. Why, that was almost as if Mama knew that she was going to die. Girlie wrote that fact in her ledger. Anyway she was glad that she had learned to pick hard and fast. She easily picked more cotton than Russel, but he always had an excuse for why. Didn't matter. All that mattered was the money. Wouldn't Lil be proud when she showed her all she'd earned and someday, maybe even Papa would be proud of her. He might even want her to come home knowing they could manage just fine.

But she'd only picked cotton for three days when it rained just enough to be too wet for picking. It kept up like that for almost a week. Molly said that idle hands is the devil's workshop, and sent her and Russel out to pick slick thistle and square weed. Molly said people had been too hoggish and cut so much poke that there wasn't any decent enough to pick. Most of it that was left had gone to berries.

Somehow it seemed a sin to be over at Molly's and not earning money. But she obeyed and picked greens until she was tired and sat down to watch the birds eating their fill of pokeberries. "Russel, you ever think how it is that birds can eat pokeberries and yet Papa says they're poison and will kill a person?"

"They wouldn't kill me. If they don't kill a little bird, they wouldn't kill me."

"Maybe they might because animals and people don't have exactly the same kinds of bodies. Papa has a big fat veterinarian book, and Mama studied it, but it was no help because animals are different. Clark Gable can eat dead mice and even rotten or moldy bread, and it don't hurt him at all. You're wrong, Russel."

"I ain't wrong, and I'll prove it." He grabbed a handful of pokeberries, and with his teeth stripped off a few berries and ate them.

"Russel, you'll die!" She had wished Russel dead a hundred times and had even told him that she would kill him if he touched Clark Gable again, but this was different. This was real.

47

"If they can't kill a little tiny bird, they can't kill me. I weigh a hundred and twenty pounds," Russel said. "Watch me for any signs of dying!"

She could feel herself begin to shake from fear, but she couldn't move. He sat there solemnly asking ever so often, "See any signs? I ain't sick yet. How do I look?"

"Russel! Puke!" Russel could throw up any time he wanted to. It was the way he always made Molly believe he was terribly sick.

"Nope, I ain't puking. I'm running a test."

No telling how long they had sat there, but it must have been a good while for Malford came looking for them. "Molly's waiting for the greens! Didn't you hear her calling and calling? What are you two doing sitting there?"

Russel straightaway told him, "We're waiting to see if I'm dying. Girlie dared me to eat pokeberries."

Before Girlie could defend herself, Malford started laughing. "Russel, you're a devil. Really had Girlie a-going, did you? Heck, Girlie, Russel's eat a bushel of pokeberries, and it ain't hurt him yet. They ain't no more poison than poke greens. Russel ain't one to believe a bunch of old folk sayings anymore than me, are you, son?"

Russel nodded. "Girlie'd believe anything. She don't know how to think."

"Which reminds me." Malford took off his cap and put it back on again. "Girlie, Mr. Cory was telling around town that Russel was the only one to get a perfect paper on them problems you helped him with. I ain't figured out how it happened, but he says you come in second by missing a half of one. Russel, did you change one of them after Girlie give you the paper?"

Russel was stopped still with a surprised look on his

48

face. Girlie was stopped still, too. But she wasn't surprised exactly; she was mad. She really wished Russel was dead now. She had changed the last half of number four, just a little bit so that Russel wouldn't get a perfect score like her. And she must have accidently made Russel's right by changing it. Russel sure had a knack for making her look dumb, even when it was an accident. Maybe she couldn't stand to stay in the house with him any longer. Maybe she ought to go back to Lil's right now, today. But she thought of Lil and of Bobby, and she knew she'd stay to get the wagon and the material for them. Money was an awfully important thing.

Russel finally stopped gawking and said, "Yeah, I guess I did change one of them answers . . . when I was copying it over. . . . I did. I changed it."

Girlie wanted to ask him, "Which one?" and expose him in his lie, but if she did she would be making herself look bad.

When Molly heard the pokeberry story, she laughed at first, and then she scolded. "Girlie, you mean you didn't come to get me and you actually believing Russel was poisoned?" She grabbed Russel and pulled him to her bosom, though he was bigger than she was, and sobbed. "Thank God it wasn't real. Girlie, I'd like to think that when there was two of you together it'd be a protection, not trouble."

Malford shook his head. "Molly, I think we made a mistake taking Girlie in. I've always heard the old folks say that put two kids together, and you've got trouble brewing."

Molly clutched Russel close again. "Thank God I chose to have only one child."

Girlie couldn't take any more. She dared not talk or she'd lose her temper again. She found her ledger and wrote carefully:

It is a fact that people can choose to not have children. Molly did. I don't blame her. Who would want two Russels? Anyway, it means that Papa chose to have me. He would never want to give me to anyone.

She felt better. At least a good knowledge came out of the bad experience. Maybe with the help of the ledger, she'd manage to stick it out here for the rest of cotton picking vacation.

In the days that followed she tried to remember that. The very next day, Russel bragged, "I can make Old Mattie charge like a bull, what do you bet I can't?"

Old Mattie was the new buck sheep Malford had gotten from the West Mattie bunch. Russel ought to have enough sense to know that animals take on the ways of the people who own them. He'd get hurt for sure messing around with that mean old sheep, and guess who would get blamed? "I ain't betting, Russel. Kill yourself if you want to, but I ain't having nothing to do with it."

Surprisingly enough, Russel didn't argue. He just walked away, and Girlie went on with some calculating, using a stick to write the figures in the sand. If she picked fifty pounds a day and if. . . .

"Watch out, watch out!" Russel was running toward her holding one of Malford's red shirts in his hand, and Old Mattie charging fast behind him.

Girlie didn't have time to jump up, so she just fell as far as she could to one side. They charged right over her legs, leaving a nasty cut from one of Old Mattie's hooves. Molly scolded them *both* for playing with the mean buck sheep.

The day after that, Russel made the geese get hissing mad until one of them bit Girlie. Molly simply said, "Put a little Hi Life on it." Hi Life was for mosquito and spider bites, not geese bites.

Then Monday morning when the Sunday *St. Louis Post-Dispatch* came in the mail, Russel grabbed the comics and told all the endings to Girlie before she had a chance to read them herself.

Every night Girlie prayed that the drizzle would let up so she could get back into the cotton patch again and make enough money to make her torture worthwhile. And Russel went right on tormenting her.

Molly insisted on at least two baths a week, and it was impossible to take one without Russel peeking and making her scream. Every Saturday her hair got washed too. Molly insisted on braiding the clean hair. Tight!

"Ouch! I don't need it braided. It hurts."

"Braid it or cut it off. Sleep on braids, and it'll comb easy as can be come morning. Now stand still. Life might be one big nice ice cream cone in your imagination, Girlie, but I'm telling you the bottom's bitten off, and the spilling is on your dress, and you're the one that will have to clean up the mess, so stand still."

She was glad to have Molly stop talking. Her teeth clicked. So as not to provoke her, Girlie stood still. Never once had she even vaguely thought that life was like a big ice cream cone. Finally Molly let her go and went after Russel to shine him to his best for church. And so ended another week.

On Sunday, the rain stopped and good cotton picking weather started again. But Russel pushed her out of the

51

car when they got home from church and caused her to cut her knee on a piece of glass. She had just about had enough of him.

She lay in wait for him on Monday as he started for the cotton field and tripped him, but he pulled her down with him, and she got the other knee skinned. For the first time she wrote in her ledger about Russel:

Russel said one of his big teeth was loosened when we fell. Molly says he gets his big teeth from Mama, though he looks like Papa.

She picked thirty-five pounds of cotton at the weighing. Russel got thirty-six. Malford was overly proud of him. He said, "Well now, Girlie, you don't need to cry. Thirty-five pounds is lots better than a peck on the head with a sharp rock."

There were no rocks handy or she might have thrown one at him, but she controlled her temper and said nothing as they went back to the house for noontime dinner.

Molly met them at the back porch with a wash pan. She stopped and stared for a moment, then she touched Russel's jaw. "Ouch!" he said. "My jaw is sore."

"You've got the mumps!" Molly cried. "Hurry and get in out of the sun or it'll raise your fever too high. Malford, give me a hand with him."

Malford was right there, helping get Russel inside the house. There was nothing that could unite Malford and Molly faster than their devotion toward Russel. It was really disgusting, putting Russel in a place for such special attention. After the trick with the pokeberries, she'd never believe again that Russel was really sick until he proved it.

"Where could you get mumps, Russel? There's nobody around here that's got them."

"Like fun there ain't. Benjie Mattie had them when I went to see him last Wednesday!"

"Russel! You didn't go inside their house, did you? They're quarantined," Malford said unbelievingly.

By the look on Russel's face, Girlie knew that he had gone inside, but he shook his head "no." "I . . . I didn't go in. Benjie came outside. I know he ain't supposed to but he came out and he stood right near me and. . . . I feel weak."

Molly and Malford moved him slowly through the back door and on into his bed, Molly crooning all the while. Well, Russel had no right to all that fuss. He was no special person, no war hero or pioneer or nothing. He was a mean kid that put paper bags on Clark Gable's feet and deliberately went into a quarantined house. And now there would be no more cotton picking with everyone quarantined inside the house. That was the law.

She hated Russel. She wished she could be glad that he had the mumps but she couldn't be, for it only meant that she too would get them. And that would stretch the quarantine even longer. She'd be forced to sit in the house and wait it out, instead of picking cotton and earning money.

Waiting was no fun. Russel threw up every time he ate and sometimes in between. He could have been doing it on purpose, but it made Molly pronounce him beastly sick. Molly brought him everything under the sun he asked for, and Malford zipped into town and bought popsicles for him.

Dr. Lester came and put the quarantine sign on the front door. A red sign with big black letters. No one could miss it. It showed up like a cherry on top of a sundae. Girlie had a sundae just once but she never forgot the delicious sweetness. Maybe if she got the mumps and couldn't hold anything down, they would try to find something to please her. Then she would tell them that she just might be able to eat an ice cream sundae if she could have one. But that would be impossible for you couldn't wrap up an ice cream sundae like a popsicle and bring it home from town. Only way she could get a sundae was to go to Betterman's Drug Store, and they'd never let her in there if she had the mumps.

Girlie sighed and felt her jaws again. Still no swelling. Maybe she'd be lucky. Wanda had never had the mumps, and she was twenty-five and had sat through three quarantines. She decided to stop feeling her throat and just hope for the best.

"Girlie," Russel yelled. "Get me something to eat. I can't wait for Ma to come back. I'm just about starving."

She went into the kitchen, opened the food safe, and got out the half-gallon fruit jar of sour pickles. She pulled out the biggest one and went back to Russel. "Russel, I'll bet this will make you yell. They say anyone with mumps can't take a single bite of pickle."

Russel raised himself disgustedly and murmured, "Give it here!" He took the pickle, took a big bite, and let the juice run from one corner of his mouth onto the best plaid blanket. Molly had piled the blanket right on top of three quilts, although it was hotter than red coals outside. Molly said it was awfully important that a sick boy with mumps stay warm, so they didn't go down on him. And when Russel said he was hot, she declared he had a fever.

54

"Molly's going to get you for dripping pickle juice on that blanket," Girlie said.

"See, it didn't hurt a bit. That's just an old wives' tale same as pokeberries being poison. But I ain't hungry. You eat the rest of it."

Chances were that that pickle wasn't all that sour. She'd been testing him without considering the fact that some jars of pickles are considerably more sour than others. She took a big bite to find out. "Help! Help! Oh, something's wrong with this pickle! My throat is burning up."

Nobody offered her sympathy. Russel started to retch loudly just as Molly got back. She had to help him through the front door so he could throw up without stinking up the whole house.

When she did finally notice Girlie, all Molly said was, "Will you stop throwing a shine and making a fuss right when I got to take care of Russel? What's this about a pickle? What's the idea of feeding Russel a pickle so's he'll throw up? Why I ought to. . . . Girlie come here." Molly reached over and felt under each side of her jaw. "You got them. Just on one side. Why didn't you tell me you was swelling?"

It was true. She must have started to swell the very minute she had decided to stop feeling her throat, because it was plenty big now.

Molly's hand was on her forehead. "No fever. That's good. You got a mild case. Thank God for small blessings. I don't know what we'd do around here with Russel so sick if we didn't have you to take care of the chores. The supper dishes got to be done, and the chickens ain't been fed yet."

"You mean . . . ?" Girlie never finished the question.

She knew no one was going to wait on her, care for her, or make nice soft interesting inquiries about how she felt. She'd been cursed with a mild case. She would not even get a popsicle, let alone a sundae.

She heard Russel calling her name. He was back in bed now, all snuggled down under his quilts and the fancy blanket that Molly lovingly tucked in about his swollen face. He was grinning! There really ought to be a law against sick people with a bad case of the mumps being allowed to grin. He said, "You got a mild case, and you can't even eat *one* bite of pickle."

Girlie didn't answer. She had some thinking to do. "Molly, if I got a half a case of mumps, will I get over them in one week?"

"Now, Girlie, you know better than that. It takes two weeks to get over the mumps whether you have them in one side or two. Of course, sometimes after two weeks, a body will come down with the other side about the time they get well from the first side."

"That's not true. That's not true!" Girlie was hating Russel more by the minute for giving her the mumps. "Nita said she just had them on one side, and she never got them on the other at all!"

"Not yet," said Molly. "But her day may still be coming. I knew a boy once that got them on one side, and never got them again until he was married and his kids were going to school. Then he got them on the other side and they almost lost him."

Girlie saw the remaining portion of the sour pickle lying on the floor where she'd dropped it. She picked it up, ran out to the back porch, and threw it out; and watched it splatter against the trunk of the elm tree. Some chickens came scurrying up to gobble up the pieces. She wished she were a chicken; no one ever heard of a chicken getting mumps! But she was no chicken; she was a girl. A most unlucky girl who got not only a mild case but only on one side. Well, one thing for sure—Russel would be wishing he'd given her a worse case by the time her two weeks were up. He'd be well during that last week, and no one would be babying and petting him, and then she'd let him have his thanks for giving her a mild case of mumps!

It didn't matter if she herself were still sick, she would let Russel have it. She was sick of sickness; she was sick of Malford and his excusing all that Russel did. She was sick of Molly talking out of one side of her mouth all lovey to Russel and out of the other side firm and tight the way she braided hair. She was going to give Russel a punch in the nose he'd never forget!

Girlie held her fist tight, but there was nothing to hit, and she had to hit, or kick, or throw. She looked for something to throw. There in a glass on the washstand were Molly's false teeth . . . guaranteed not to break. It'd be almost as good as socking someone in the mouth. She picked them out of the glass and started to throw them, but on second thought climbed upon a chair first so she could really throw them with the force she felt. WHAM!

"Girlie!" There stood Russel in the doorway, the plaid blanket wrapped around him and his mouth slack with disbelief. On the floor lay Molly's teeth in three sections, not two. The lowers had *broken*!

Girlie stood on the chair as if her feet were glued tight to it, and she couldn't move. She watched Russel disappear and heard him screaming, "Great balls of cat hair, Girlie has gone crazy! Ma! Paw!"

Her feet came unglued, and she leaped from the porch and started running toward Black River. She was leaving

Molly's . . . without her belongings . . . without her cotton picking money. At the thought of the money the weight of her act hit her. How could she go back to Lil without having done what she'd left to do? She wasn't even bringing back the little money she had earned! Lil might even hate her for breaking Molly's teeth. How could she have done such a terrible thing? It was her temper; she'd lost her temper again. Papa was right not to want such a terrible person around his house.

She tramped on down to the river's edge. There would be no more cotton picking money this season, no wagon for Bobby, no bought dress material for Lil. She was weary from it all. She was weary from the running. Her pulse beat wildly in her swollen neck. There was no other way she could earn money. There simply would be no more money. The words "no more, no more" beat in her head. She was sick but had to keep going, just like Mama.

When Mama died the whisperings said things like, No more. . . . No more. . . . No more. "It was a blessing she died. Some women get sick like that and go around for years and years. Working . . . suffering. Working . . . suffering. Thirteen years of suffering. It was a relief to her. A blessing she died. She wouldn't want to stay alive and bear up under it like it was."

Now Girlie understood what it was to be sick and never get to quit and give into it. Oh, it was a dread disease that put Mama on Sand Hill. A slow killer. Not bad enough to get her help and comfort, just work and suffering. Could Girlie have it right this minute and not know it? Is that what made her get mumps so differently than Russel, and people push her aside instead of love her when she was sick? She waded out into the water. The mud on the bottom was soft. The drizzles of the past week had caused the river to rise only a bit, and the water never got higher than her armpits. And getting wet certainly beat walking the four miles around if she'd taken the bridge.

Clark Gable hissed at her when she pushed Lil's front door open. But he got over it right away. Girlie picked him up and started crooning to him.

And then Lil was hugging them both. "Oh Girlie, what has happened. Tell me honey. What has happened?"

Symond said, "Dry yourself off, Girlie. I'll get a quilt for your cot."

As fast as she could, she told Lil what she had done. Lil never said it was good or bad, she just listened. So did Symond. All her talking woke Bobby. He came into the front room, staring with big haunty eyes, then he cried, "Girlie! Girlie, I made the moon stand still. I stopped running and it stopped running."

"Sure you did, Bobby." Oh Bobby was such a dear little fellow. She hugged him to her wet body. She remembered when she and Nita had once eaten dirt because Papa had said, "We all eat over a pound a year." It was years later that she learned Papa had meant it as a joke. Childhood was nice. In a way it was nice that Bobby would forever be a child.

She laughed and asked, "Lil, can I have a towel now? I need to go to sleep."

They left her to dry and bed down. She moved the cot so it sat just beneath the front room window. With the light off and only the moon glow in the window, it seemed that she was home upstairs in the bed she and Nita shared. The sky looked the same the world over, changing but always familiar. She snuggled up to Clark Gable and fell asleep to the sound of his deep purring.

She woke late the next morning. Lil and Bobby were

outside; she could hear them talking. She walked out to the back porch half asleep and washed her face. Then moved on out to join Lil and Bobby on the steps and find out what to expect next.

"You sure got a shiny nose, Girlie," Bobby said.

Lil hardly looked up from her chore of scrubbing Bobby's feet. She looked pale.

Girlie said, "It's hot, and I'm sweaty, Bobby. Besides, I got the mumps and Molly made my braids too tight. My nose always shines when the skin is stretched too tight. I'm aiming to take out these braids and comb my hair straight right now. I ain't at Molly's no more."

Suddenly Lil jumped from the back porch steps and out to the weed patch to begin violently retching. Girlie dropped the big wide-toothed comb she was using and ran to help. "Oh, Lil, you're sick. I just knew it. I just knew it. I've given you the mumps again."

"Yeah, and I knew it, too." Lil had a sad wry smile as she sat down on a hill of black dirt which Bobby called his toad house. "Yeah, I knew it, but it ain't the mumps. All of us here have had them."

"What you smiling about? It ain't funny to be sick. I don't smile because I got the mumps. It hurts anyway when I laugh."

"This hurts too, Girlie, but I ain't really sick. You don't call being pregnant sick."

For a moment Girlie began to smile in spite of her mumps, she was so delighted with the good news. But then she saw Lil's eyes. She was silently crying. She'd never seen Lil cry about anything. "Lil don't you want a nice little baby? Bobby's seven, and you ought to have another one."

"No, honey, I oughten to have another one. I love Sy-

60

mond, he's good and he loves me more than anyone has a right to be loved. He's not dumb, maybe just a little slow on some things, but it don't matter if you're plowing whether you can do a math problem or not, but I never thought about our children. I never thought it possible that our children might come up a little worse off, like my sweet happy Bobby who'll never even worry about what he don't know. Symond's not real slow like his two brothers but our little Bobby is. Bobby needs a lot of watching and a lot of love. No, Girlie, I oughten to have another one, but it kind of looks like I'm going to." Lil had that strange smile again.

Girlie remembered the fact she had written in her ledger. "But you don't have to have a baby if you don't want it. Molly chose not to have any more after Russel."

"That's almost true, honey, but nothing is perfect as they say. Thank God it worked for Mama, it give her a few more years of life and a chance to raise you. And so far it's worked for Molly whatever her reasons are. I want this baby, Girlie. I really do. But I want it to be strong and bright. I want it to be a pretty little long-haired girl like you was, all aglow with life and big eyes eager to see and understand the world. I want to make her pretty little dresses like Mama sewed for us. I want to have the ways and means to provide. . . ." Lil was crying again. "Girlie, I wanted you to be educated proper and to wear clothes of store-bought material. I've stretched my means now until the story of the loaves and fishes looks like beginners' triflings."

"I'll work. I'll go back to Molly's right this minute. I'll work hard. First I'll pay for Molly's teeth. Then I'll get Bobby one of them little toy wagons, and then I'll get lots of store-bought material. . . ."

"Honey, honey, honey. You don't have any idea how much all that would cost. At Molly's you'd only add to the length of their quarantine. It's all right. I ain't crying. You can look at me now, Girlie. Mama told me once if I wanted a thing, all I had to do was set my mind on it, and the Lord would provide the ways and means. . . ."

"I know. Mama told me that too."

"Only what I want, even God can't change. I'll show you in my library book. It's inheritance. Like eye color and hair color. My baby has a chance of being bright. I got to remember that. It's got a chance. You see, Girlie, I don't want to stop loving Symond. I took my chances with my eyes open."

Girlie wasn't sure she understood all of what Lil was saying. Lil didn't *have* to stop loving Symond. No one was making her. Girlie didn't want to show her own dumbness by asking any further questions. She just said, "You'll have a sweet baby, Lil."

Lil said, "I'll have a baby, and that's a fact that I can't prevent now. What one can't prevent there ain't no use crying over, now is there, Girlie? And it will be sweet, and I will love it and we'll manage. We always have. There now, thanks for letting your big sister cry on your shoulder. Come on now, as Papa always says, 'We got work to do.' And some thinking and planning for you. I talked about it some to Symond this morning before you woke up. We got to get your things from Molly's. Maybe Symond can get some kind of swap work for you to do during cotton picking vacation. He's pretty good at swapping. He is for a fact."

Girlie helped Lil can vegetable soup from the sacks and baskets of garden stuff he'd got by swapping with other men's wives who had an overabundance. They barely got

62

the last jar sealed before Symond got home and they had to start supper. Bobby had been begging for supper for an hour, but they couldn't afford to stop to feed him. Now Clark Gable had joined in the hungry cry, and he wouldn't settle for a raw carrot the way Bobby had.

When Symond finished washing his face for supper he paused as if to let the cooling water penetrate. Girlie knew he was enjoying the good wetness and she smiled. Symond smiled back for one second, before he hid his face in the towel and said, "Girlie, I called Malford. Him and Molly will be over tonight after supper to settle all this business." Then his face all dried he said, "I'm hungry as Clark Gable. I guess we better get at it. They'll be over before we know it."

They did come before the last yeasty bun had sopped up the last of the bean juice on their plates. It wasn't right to leave food, so while Lil's family sopped, Molly's family talked. Russel had come along, too.

Malford said, "I ain't calling names, but someone has caused us a lot of worry and now has caused us to break the law by defying a quarantine and leaving the house to come over here."

Russel and Molly were nodding their heads in firm agreement. Girlie felt like screaming. She felt like telling them that no one could live with them and not cause trouble. She felt like telling them that their house ought to be quarantined forever. But she took another bite of sopped bread instead and swallowed her temper. She didn't want to be bad again.

Molly said, "It's got to be clear as day to you that we can't keep Girlie on. Lil, I'm sorry for the money's sake, and I know we made a bargain with you but what's not right is not right. Russel's swelling is going down and him and Malford can be picking again in a couple of days. Girlie won't hold a thing up staying here with you. There's no reason to call the sheriff because you only have to report when someone comes down with them, and she did that at my house."

Russel said, "Lil couldn't call the sheriff nohow. She ain't got no phone."

Malford said, "That's right, son. Now me and Molly talked this over and talking ain't exactly easy for her, just wearing her uppers. Lil, Symond, we know you folks can't keep Girlie cause you ain't got the means. And we can't keep her because she spells trouble. The old saying of putting two kids together and you brew trouble is sure true if Girlie is one of them. Well, I did what a self-respecting family member would do. I called on another member of the family to take her. I called Rose over in Poplar Bluff because her man Parker does make fair money from his house painting jobs. He's gone a lot which is more reason why Rose might welcome company around. Parker Junior ain't big enough to fight with nobody, and I heard that in that Poplar Bluff school they got a set-up called Diversified Occupation where a girl can work part time and earn a little money while she goes to school."

"And Girlie ought to pay for her keep at Rose's, else Parker would take a dim view," Molly added. She didn't sound too bad without her lowers, a little lispy but no clicks. "I ain't asking her to pay for my teeth, because they're guaranteed. Anyway, Rose called me back to say that the D.O. program don't start until high school and Girlie can't go. But I wasn't born oldest in this family without learning that first answers don't necessarily mean last answers. I just called up Martha Mattie who works at the school and told her my problem. In no time flat, Martha called me back saying she talked to the superintendent, and it's all fixed. My phone bill's going to be a big one, but I ain't asking no help in paying it. I'm your sister, Lil . . . and yours too, Girlie."

Girlie had listened while all the talking took place but she hadn't really had time to start feeling what all those words meant. They meant that she would have to leave Lil's. She looked at Lil and Symond. Lil was still sopping her plate, though it was dry as a warm stove lid. Symond was helping Bobby manage his last bite of beans. Then they looked at each other, and Lil nodded. Symond whispered, "You'll be in a right pretty place at Rose's."

So she was to be sent to live at Rose's at Poplar Bluff. It made her angry to have Lil and Symond agree . . . and so fast too. She clenched her teeth to hold back her temper. Then she saw the anxious look on Lil's face and knew that if she asked to stay Lil would let her. She said, "I guess I'm real lucky to get to live in town."

Quickly Lil said, "You'll go to a big school, and they got a library there. You know—where Martha Mattie gets all the good books she's been bringing us."

"And you can get in that work program at the school," Molly added. "I think it'd be right interesting myself to work in a dry-goods store."

Girlie didn't know what to say. Yet they all sat there waiting for her to say something. She said, "I don't know how to work in a dry-goods store."

Molly smiled. "That's what they teach you as part of your schooling. They teach you how to sell. Well . . . it's getting dark; we ought to be going Malford. Russel, honey, run and get Girlie's things out of the car."

Girlie ran after Russel; she didn't want him spilling out

her underthings or something like that. Russel grabbed her pillowcase and held it up with his right hand, in his left he held up her ledger. "Hey Girlie, you got some interesting things in this old book."

She snatched it from him and ran back to the house away from them all. She stood in the doorway and listened to the good-byes. Molly was saying, "It's all right, Lil. It's only fair that Rose does her share. It ain't right that one person get stuck with it all."

The words went deep and the hurt filled her. She was just some thing that others got stuck with. Comfort came in the form of a furry caress against her legs. She reached down and picked up Clark Gable. When Lil and Symond came back in, she whispered her hope, "You think Rose will let me bring Clark Gable?"

"Sure, sure, honey. Rose wouldn't make you leave your pet behind," Lil whispered back.

Symond said, "It's been a hard day for you, Girlie. Don't worry now. Go to bed and get some sleep."

Bobby repeated, "Don't worry now. Get some sleep."

Girlie gave Bobby a hug, and then Lil was there hugging them both. "Girlie, it's all right. Don't fight new experiences. It's all a part of life's learnings. We best all go to bed now."

As soon as Lil's little family had settled in the next room, Girlie reached up and pulled the electric light on for one minute while she wrote in her ledger:

Correction of a fact. Sometimes people get babies they don't want.

five

GIRLIE had to say good-bye to Symond and Lil and Bobby at their house for it was in Malford's car that she was to go to Rose's. Molly rode along, but Russel didn't, thank goodness. It was the first time Clark Gable had ever ridden in a car, and he was hard enough to handle without having Russel along to make matters worse.

Malford said, "Girlie, that cat of yourn is going to get you in a peck of trouble one of these days. See if you can't get him a little quieter. We're pulling in at Rose's, and we can do without all that racket. We're in town now."

The minute the car stopped, Clark Gable stopped his yowing too, so Malford had no need to worry. Girlie got out holding the cat closely in her arms. Rose came to meet them carrying Parker Jr. who was clutching a tiny white curly-haired puppy.

Rose's first words were, "We can't have that cat in the house."

"I can't keep Clark Gable?"

"You can keep him. I didn't say you couldn't. But we got Curly in the house for Parker Junior to play with. Cats and dogs fight. Come on around back, and I'll show you where your cat can sleep."

Molly said, "That's sure a pretty dress you got on, Rose."

Rose tilted her head and said, "Aw, this old rag." But her walk showed that she was pleased.

They all followed Rose through a bed of mums that were almost hidden by weeds, then on around to a little shelter underneath an outside stairway. "This is the stairs coming out of our place, so it'll be all right for your cat to sleep here. Go out to the trash and find a box. I'll get you some old rags."

Molly said, "If any of them rags is like what you're wearing, I'll take them myself."

Girlie took Clark Gable to help find the right-sized box. Rose was saying, "I hope it ain't bad luck to come in through the back door on your visit Molly," as she led the others up the stairs.

"Never fear," said Molly. "Getting that cat settled is the important thing. Boy, I thought I'd go crazy. . . ."

The back door of Rose's apartment slammed, and now Girlie could really talk to Clark Gable and explain without being laughed at. "Clark, I'll make sure this box will keep you warm and dry, and I'll come outside all the time and talk to you. It won't be for long. I'm going to be so good here at Rose's that word of it will soon get back to Papa, and he'll come and take us home. He's sure to be here for us before cold weather sets in."

The box was a good size, and Rose came out with a big

mess of rags. Malford and Molly followed. Malford said, "We can't stay. Got work to do and Lord knows what Russel is up to. Girlie, don't take any wooden nickels at that store and take care of that cat of yourn."

Rose said, "She'll have to. Honestly, I don't know whatever made her pick up that scrawny animal that night at the movie show. It was homely then, and it's still homely. It'd be understandable her being crazy over a cute pet like Curly. But everybody to their own likes, I reckon."

"I reckon!" Girlie snapped. "At least my cat has a real name and not just a description like curly. Everyone and everything has a right to have a good solid name."

Molly said, "Now Girlie, control that temper of yourn. That ain't no way to start out. Of course I can sympathize with you some on this looks business. All my life I had to stand back and hear people ask Mama, 'Mary, ain't it sad that some of your other girls didn't turn out pretty as Rose?' They'd say it right in front of me as if I didn't have ears. But I don't expect you'd understand them feelings Rose."

Rose said, "Looks ain't everything. I won that beauty contest at the pie supper where they paid a penny a vote, but it didn't do me no good. I never got that job selling in the store like I wanted. Now Girlie here is going to get to sell in a store, and her with no looks to speak of. Times have changed. I'm glad for her though."

Molly was quick to agree. "We all are. Five dollars a month ain't being rich, but it's good pay for part-time and it'll be year-round. Your Parker was good enough to say that five dollars was just fine for her keep, and it will be a help to you on the grocery bill. I know food's expensive in town. Of course we didn't charge her a dime. What

69

cotton picking money she earned Malford give her to keep; give it to her before we made the trip over this morning."

That reminded Girlie to check to see that her belongings were safe. They were still there by the stairs. The $3.13 from picking was tucked in between the pages in her ledger.

Parker Jr. was crying at the head of the stairs. Molly and Malford said they really ought to leave and did. Rose called to Girlie as she walked patiently up to get Parker Jr., "Girlie you come on in. Bring your belongings, and I'll show you to your room."

Girlie gave Clark Gable one last caress, grabbed up her pillowcase of belongings, and followed Rose. The stairs led right into the fanciest kitchen she'd ever seen, with brown and yellow built-in cabinets from ceiling to floor.

Rose led the way straight into the living room, where she put Parker Jr. and Curly into a little fenced-in corner. "Just put your things in the closet. I'll be with you in a minute."

There was a row of doors about four feet high to one side of the living room. Girlie opened one.

"No, no, Girlie, that's not a closet. That's just an old junk hole back there under the eaves."

"Rose, there's a doll in here. My gosh, where did you get all this?" She'd never seen so many toys: dolls, a wagon, roller skates, small furniture. It seemed as if every Christmas that Girlie had ever dreamed of lay in a jumbled heap inside these short closet doors. She pulled out the largest doll and cradled it carefully.

Rose's pretty little round face moved to look more firm as she said in her slow soft voice, "Better put it back. They told me this was storage and not to be touched. It belongs

70

to the people who own this house and used to live in it before they turned it into apartments."

Girlie put the big doll back. It was a sin to have pretty toys all hidden away and getting dusty. Of course she herself wouldn't want to play with them. She was twelve and that is certainly too old to play with toys. But wouldn't Bobby love to play with that wagon there? She held the door ajar for another few seconds just to look. There was no harm in looking. Surely the people wouldn't object to anyone just looking. She closed the door reluctantly. When Rose called from another room.

"Here, Girlie, here's your closet. In here in your room."

"My room?"

"It's yours, such as it is. Not much more than a big old storage closet itself with a little peeping window, but it fits a bed," Rose said and then added, "I'm going to make us a pie."

The room was just the right size to hold a small bed. Back under the eaves were closet doors again like the ones in the living room. Girlie hung up her dresses and the red satin blouse that Lil had made on the little rod. She placed her other things in a neat pile on the floor and went out to the kitchen to see if she could be of help with the pie.

Rose took out a large blue enameled pie tin, flour, and a quart-sized sifter that still looked brand new, even though she and Parker had been married for three years.

"You making a lemon pie?" Girlie asked. "Papa says you make the best lemon pies he ever ate."

"No, I ain't. I ain't making no more lemon pies ever. After that awful shine Parker made the last time, I'd be caught dead first. I want Parker to like my cooking. He just don't care for lemons of any sort, so I've took to doing what he does like. I'm making coconut cream. I'll make some other kinds for you too, while Parker's gone, but I'll never make another lemon. If I made lemon, it'd just be my luck that that'd be the day Parker would come home and catch me."

"You get to make pies any time you want to?"

"I do. Sometimes I make out my meal on nothing but pie. Parker likes to make me happy. Of course I like to make him happy, too. He wanted you to stay with me if that's what I wanted. To be company when he's gone, which is often enough as it is. Seems like every single painting job is miles away from here."

"Rose, I'm grateful he let me come stay. I'm grateful."

"Girlie, you *ought* to feel grateful that Parker was kind-hearted enough to let you come live with us so you can go to a big town school. Town schools has lots of things that little country schools don't have. Tomorrow you first go to your Diversified Occupation class and get taught how to do your new job, and then they'll actually hire you out to that kind of job."

"Molly said I was already hired out. She said she fixed it so I already had the job in a dry-goods store."

"Wasn't Molly. It was that Martha Mattie. She was sure hoping she could get you the job. The teacher of D.O. said that most storekeepers who took part in the job program expected ninth graders and girls at least fourteen years old, but he'd see what he could do. Then Martha Mattie said, 'Girlie must be a pretty talented one to be in eighth grade at age twelve.' Then the D.O. teacher said, 'I'll sure see what I can do to convince them of that,' and he did it."

Girlie didn't feel talented. Certainly she wasn't talented in finding a real home for herself, a place where she really belonged and could stay until such time as she was ready for grown-up life.

She watched as Rose made the coconut cream pie, rolling the crust a few strokes and stopping for a drink of coke and then rolling some more. It took half a bottle of coke for her to get the crust rolled out to a perfect roundness and the other half to see her through the slow stirring of the cream filling. Then Rose opened a new bottle of coke, while she waited for the crust and filling to cool. Rose never hurried with anything in life. Girlie watched as Rose took slow, almost dainty, sips of the coke. Rose was soft and pretty like her name, and she no more belonged in a hurried place than a delicate rose belonged in a wind storm.

"What you staring at, Girlie? That ain't polite."

"I'm sorry. I guess I was just watching you drink your coke. I didn't mean to stare."

"Why ain't you drinking one? Don't you like coke?"

"Rose, you never told me I could have any. I figured maybe you was saving it for Parker."

"Parker don't like coke. He buys it for me. He's not coming home for a month anyway. I got ten cases of soda pop stuck under the inside stair steps. You can have a coke whenever you want it. Good gosh, Girlie, I don't care if you drink coke. If I didn't have my coke, I'd die, I guess."

The truth was that Girlie didn't like coke. During cotton picking time and on the Fourth of July and when Uncle Bob came to visit, she always chose orange or maybe one of the little tiny Grapettes. She preferred the Grapette but the orange lasted longer. The idea of ten cases of soda pop being in someone's house all at one time was hard to believe, but Rose wasn't lying. There really were ten cases when Girlie went to get a bottle from under the stair steps that led to the apartment downstairs. She chose Green River with its marvelous lemony-lime flavor.

Girlie drank the soda pop and Rose looked pleased. "We got that Green River for Parker Junior's bottle."

She had begun mixing the cream filling with coconut when Parker Jr. let out with some loud screams. Girlie ran to his little fenced-in corner. She found that Curly had squeezed out through the fence, and the baby was screaming to get him back. Girlie picked him up and bounced him up and down until he started giggling. She held him in the air with her hands around his fat little stomach and wiggled him good.

"Parker Junior, you're a monkey. You're a funny little monkey. You stand there screeching like that, you looked just like Bobby when he can't have his way."

Suddenly Rose grabbed Parker Jr. There was nothing slow about her actions this time or her words. "Don't you never say that my baby looks like that ape Bobby. My baby ain't retarded. I don't care what Lil put in your head, being born crazy ain't hereditary. It comes from being marked or injured or something before the baby's born. Don't you ever mention Bobby around this house again. You mention it one time in front of Parker, and you'll have to leave. I don't want you to ever feel you're not welcome, but you'd have to leave."

"I'm sorry Rose. I didn't mean nothing. I like Bo . . . I mean, I didn't mean it as an insult. Everybody knows that Parker Junior ain't slow. Why he's the cutest and smartest little boy in the whole world! Let me hold him Rose. See, he wants to come to me."

Rose relaxed, handed Parker Jr. to Girlie, and they

went back into the kitchen and ate coconut pie and drank more soda.

Rose said, "It's all right to eat as much pie as you want. It makes me feel good to have my cooking appreciated."

So Girlie ate half the pie and Rose the rest except for the small amount they fed to Parker Jr. Curly and Clark Gable had to eat the leavings of the chocolate pudding that Rose had made at noon. Girlie ate so much that she did something she had never done before. She didn't quite finish a bottle of soda pop, so she hid it in her little bedroom. She would finish it later when her stomach settled down from all the rich eating.

But later, when she went to crawl into her bed, she made a discovery. The soda pop had lost its bubbles. Now that was something learned today! She got out her ledger and wrote down the new fact. It had nothing to do with Mama's death but it was interesting and should be recorded:

Pop loses bubbles if you let it sit.

No bottle of pop had ever sat in her home long enough to see that happen. This was a new world she was in and she'd be learning lots of new things.

She made sure the door was closed before she pulled off her dress. She slept in her panties and slip. Sometimes they got a little stinky before wash day, but she had to stay dressed decent even at night for no one ever had a lock on a door. Sometimes she wished there were locks, for her breasts were beginning to form and she was afraid that people might notice even if she did have her slip on. Rose might come in to sit on the bed and chat at night.

Rose didn't come, so Girlie turned her eyes toward the bare rafters of this small room that was snuggled under the eaves and said her prayer. She always looked upward when she talked to God. She'd learned that from Mama. When she was a very, very small girl, she'd lie on the pallet by Mama's feet in church and watch her as she looked at the church rafters and sang, "When the Roll Is Called Up Yonder, I'll Be There." It was like Mama was talking straight to God. At that time Girlie even believed God lived up under the roof of the church. Now she knew that Mama had been thinking of Heaven, and it was almost as if Mama had known she was going to die and was practicing conversing with God in person.

An awful racket cut right into her thoughts. It was Clark Gable and he was in the house! Girlie ran to the living room to find Curly yelping and Clark Gable growling.

She grabbed Clark and started toward the back door scolding as she went, "I'm ashamed of you, Clark. That little puppy is scared of you. You're twice his size. Oh, so that's how you got in."

There was a hole in the corner of the back screen door. She pushed Clark out and closed the regular door this time.

Rose was standing there in a pink satin nightgown. "We'll roast alive tonight with that back door closed. Can't you make that cat of yourn mind?"

Girlie shook her head. "That hole is asking for trouble. It's a wonder Curly hadn't already found it himself and gone running out into the night."

She reached down and picked up Curly and began to pet him. "Poor little fellow. You don't have to be scared. And you don't have to worry about being chased by any big animals. . . ." What was she saying? The "big animal" was her very own Clark Gable. She put Curly down and snuck out the back door and called, "Here Clark, here Clark. HERE CLARK, HERE, CLARK."

A gruff voice shouted, "Will you cut out the noise up there! Let a body sleep!"

That must be the man who lived downstairs. It had never occurred to her not to yell. Why on the farm you always yelled if you wanted your pet.

She whispered, "Here Clark, come on Clark." Suddenly there was Clark curling himself around her legs. "Oh, please get in your bed and let me get back to mine before that man comes raging out and finds me in my under-slip."

She quickly tucked him into his box and ran back to hop into her own bed.

She slept poorly. And the whole next day was a blur of one strangeness on top of another. The school was big, made of red bricks with marble slabs by the front entrance. There were so many classrooms she had to ask question after question, and finally ended up in the principal's office. He got her a schedule and showed her around. That afternoon the D.O. teacher went with her to the dry-goods store to meet her boss, Mr. Krendall. He told her so many things she couldn't even remember them all to repeat them to Rose that night. She only knew one thing for sure, she was to sell baby clothes, and she was tired.

After a couple of weeks the days took on a pattern of school classes in the morning and selling baby clothes in the afternoon. The pattern had its strangeness that was hard to get used to, like all the fancy clothes that the girls wore to school. They wore a different dress everyday! She wore her good school dress for the first three days, and then she starched up her everyday dress and wore that to school too, and finally she wore her yellow Sunday dress. That was the day she noticed that boys here acted differently toward her too.

One boy in particular, Dobe Tyler, was awfully friendly. She sat next to him in math class, where you were seated according to your grades. The best in the back right-hand corner seat and next best in the next seat and so on. Either she or Dobe sat in the best seat or the one next to it, like they were taking turns.

She worked hard at school to keep her grades high, and she worked hard at the store for the money and also because she found she had some ideas about selling she wanted to carry out. She was almost too tired at the end of the day to appreciate the wonderful chocolate, raisin, or burnt-sugar pies that Rose made for their supper. Sometimes she couldn't finish her half of the pie and had to sneak the rest out to the garbage, so as not to hurt Rose's feelings. But as tired as she was at night, it was difficult to fall asleep because she missed Clark Gable's warm furry presence and the chance to confide in him. It's painful to have your head full of new things and big ideas, and no one to talk to.

One day, when she got home, Rose said, "If you don't mind staying here and sleeping in my room near Parker Junior, I'm going to take in a movie. You're no company going to bed so early like you do. I've a mind to see Gabby Hayes at the Rialto. Parker Junior used to sleep right through a movie but he's got so he can't do it, now that he's older."

"Sure, Rose. I don't mind a bit."

She lay down on Rose's bed on the pillowcase that said

HERS. It was pink satin and had little roses embroidered on the edge. The other pillowcase matched except it said HIS in the middle surrounded by oil stain from Parker's Wildroot Creme Oil. One thing Girlie was not about to do was to use Parker's pillow. She fell asleep that night feeling troubled and not exactly welcome in Rose's home.

The next day at the dry-goods store she had two surprises. First Darnella came in. She'd seen Rose at the Rialto the night before and found out that Girlie was staying in Poplar Bluff. Darnella lived in Poplar Bluff herself. She and Galen had found a little place at the edge of town she said. When Mr. Krendall saw her visiting on company time, Darnella had to leave, but she promised to come by some evening.

The second surprise was Mr. Krendall bringing a man over who wanted to talk to her. This time he said it was all right to use company time to do the visiting. It seemed this Mr. Hobler manufactured dresses and was interested in the one she was wearing. That was a day for wearing her embroidered yellow dotted swiss, and she was proud to tell him her Mama had made it.

"Your Mama made it?" Mr. Hobler looked at her face in a strange and careful way. "You are the daughter of Mary Webster? Of course you are. I see you are."

"Mama is dead now."

Mr. Hobler looked away for a moment, and when he looked back his face was tight and he forced his words, "Your mother made the dress you're wearing?"

"Yes, and she made a blue one just like it for Nita. Darnella's was of a different pattern because she's taller."

"Miss Webster, could I make a deal with you? You let me borrow that dress of yours for a couple of weeks to get the pattern, and I'll give you twenty-five dollars and any new dress from the line I sell Mr. Krendall here. Is it a deal?"

At first Girlie couldn't answer, until she saw by his face that he was serious. He had a nice face. Smooth and brown and free with smile lines that touched his black hair. He must be Papa's age, but he didn't look as old or weary. He smiled again as if waiting for her answer. She nodded her head yes.

"Then go back and choose your dress and change in the dressing room. I'll make it all right with Mr. Krendall, don't worry."

She chose a soft green woolen dress. It was a little hot for right now but that didn't matter one bit. It had pearl buttons.

Mr. Hobler smiled pleasantly. "You've excellent taste young lady, very like your mother. Do you like your work here?"

"Yes, now that I'm getting things straight. I think I'm going to really like it, soon's I get to try out a couple of ideas I got. Pretty things ain't always the things that cost the most you know, and there's lots of farm women that would love to get one or two store-bought things for their baby. . . . I figure that Mr. Krendall could make a profit if I could pick out the prettiest things, that were reasonable, of course, and then if he'd just mark them down a little bit more than usual." What was she doing? She was rattling on to this strange man telling all the ideas she'd been dying to discuss with someone. She dropped her head so she wouldn't have to look him in the eye.

"Don't stop, go on. You've a mind of a business woman and the good taste of a designer. You know, Miss Webster, women have made themselves good careers in retailing. I run into them often in my business."

He waited for her to speak but she couldn't think of what to say. After a couple seconds he said, "Don't you stop your plans. Now I'd better give you your money and be on my way." He handed her two tens and a five. She could hardly wait to show Rose.

But Rose wasn't home when she got there. There was only a note saying Parker was back and was taking her and Parker Jr. out for hamburgers and a movie. How she wished they had waited for her. Didn't Rose know that she had never eaten a hamburger in her whole life, that Papa killed hogs not beef? Here she was wearing a new dress, the owner of twenty-five dollars, the recipient of great compliments, and not a soul to share her good fortune with. She ought to be having a party and telling everyone the wonderful news. Why not? She'd have one all by herself. Excitement ran through her as she looked at her fine dress in the mirror of Rose's dresser. Curly was yipping and jumping being excited with her, but she really wanted Clark Gable. Well, Rose wasn't home to stop her from bringing him in.

First she put Curly in Rose's room and closed the door; then she went downstairs and got Clark Gable; then she went into the living room and opened the door that concealed the toys. She took them out one by one and placed them around the living room. Four dolls, one table, two chairs, one dainty vanity just about the right size for little Susy, and a pair of roller skates with pom poms on the lace. A little red wagon! Oh, if only she had Bobby here. She placed the four dolls on the two chairs and drew them up to the table.

81

"Please girls, wait right here until I bring out the food for our party."

She made a large onion sandwich with a lot of salt, cut it into small pieces, and brought it to the little table. She had to sit on the little red wagon, but she did it with dignity. Clark Gable sat next to her. "Oh, this dress? You want to know where I got it? Well, first I have to tell you about this nice man, Mr. Hobler, who has a smile that just makes a person feel good. . . ."

So busy was she with her talk that she didn't hear the sounds on the stairs. The door flew open and there was Darnella exclaiming over seeing Girlie, and then over the dress and the toys. Behind her was Rose and Parker holding Parker Jr.

Rose started to shout but Parker stopped her. "Let her just try to tell us what she is doing."

Rose ran to her bedroom door and jerked it open, letting Curly join the show. Girlie grabbed up Clark Gable and tried to hold him while he hissed and clawed against her new dress. Darnella grabbed Clark and put him outside, then said, "Calm down, honey, tell us what this is all about."

Girlie told them about Mr. Hobler and how he wanted her dress for a pattern and how he gave her this dress for the use of hers. She didn't tell about the twenty-five dollars. At that moment she decided the money would be hers for emergency use only. When a person has that much, she is never completely helpless. She didn't try to explain the toys. She just said, "I'm sorry."

Parker shook his head and said, "I'm right sorry too. Mighty sorry. I can't have you causing my wife trouble. I can't have you sneaking around and doing what you've been told not to do. Bringing that cat in the house! Hauling out other people's belongings! You'll get us evicted. Rose, I think we got us a lemon here. Go change that dress, Girlie! *Rose* can't even afford a dress like that!"

Darnella said, "No, Girlie, don't change your pretty new dress. You just go get your belongings, and you can wear that pretty new dress right over to my house. Galen is waiting outside. He'll carry your stuff."

Girlie got her things together so fast that she had no time to write in her ledger, but she would record the facts of this matter later. It seemed that all she did lately was move, move, move, and she needed to get the reason straight.

six

GALEN was there waiting when Darnella and Girlie came downstairs with Girlie's belongings.

Darnella said, "Galen, I just couldn't leave Girlie in the same house with Parker. He's so jealous, it's sinful. Girlie can sleep out on the cot on our porch until cold weather sets in."

Galen said, "Hand me her sack. If Girlie wants to sleep on our porch, then she can sleep on our porch."

"Can you wait a minute? I got to find Clark Gable." She started calling, "HERE CLARK, HERE CLARK. . . ." Then she remembered how late it was and started hunting quietly. Clark had heard though and found her at once. She picked him up and started the three-mile walk to Darnella's house. She was still wearing her new dress and hidden deep in her pillowcase was her extra twenty-five dollars. It wouldn't be too bad living with Darnella.

She could still keep her job and go to her school. She was grateful for that.

They walked along beneath the street lights and when a block was so long that the darkness deepened, Galen turned on his flashlight.

Galen said, "What's the matter Girlie that you ain't talking? The cat got your tongue?"

Girlie didn't answer that awful question for fear of what she might say. Nor did she think on it, for the very thought was gory. It made her sure that she didn't care for Galen.

Galen said, "I know what we can do to get you loosened up a little. What say Darnella, we get her a cherry ice cream soda at Marx's?"

Darnella put her arm around Galen and gave him a hug, and he bent close to her and whispered into her ear and then howled with glee when she said, "Quit it, now quit it, Galen."

But they did take her to Marx's. It was a place to behold. The man behind the long marble counter asked what they'd like. She placed Clark Gable on the floor under her tall round stool, and then looked around to see what they had.

Galen said, "I'll take a double hamburger," he winked at Darnella. "No onions. And two cherry sodas and that'll do her."

The man threw two balls of meat on a flat metal stove and smashed them with a long egg-turner. Then he took two tulip-shaped tall glasses from a shelf and dropped a scoop of ice cream in the bottom of each. He poured some red syrup over that, and then pulled a little lever that made water come shooting out with great power hissing like mad, making the ice cream and syrup bubble a mile high. He dug out another big hunk of ice cream and dropped in right in the middle of the bubbles, and then stuck a straw and a tall spoon down along side that last ball of ice cream and set them on the counter. Darnella pushed one toward Girlie and kept the other for herself.

Girlie always thought she would like to taste a hamburger, but right now she was willing to forget everything except the soda. This was the best tasting thing she had ever had. She looked at herself in the great mirror that was along the wall behind the man. What a pretty sight! Her in her soft green dress and that bubbly cherry soda. She kept sucking on the straw until it made a gurgling sound and Darnella frowned, then she finished it off with the long spoon. Galen paid the man forty-five cents, and they continued on with their journey.

"Thank you," Girlie said, "but I can pay for my own if you want me to."

"Keep your money," Galen slapped her on the back. "I got a good job with the carnival this week. We can live it up, right, Darnella?" He gave Darnella a slap on the rear.

"Stop it, Galen, I said, stop it. Girlie's my little sister."

"Well what do you know, Girlie? Want to know a way to have lots of friends?"

Girlie didn't quite know how to answer Galen. She hadn't been around him very much when he hired out to Papa. So she didn't know him all that well. She'd never heard him talk so much. "I guess so," she answered.

"Well, do like the worms do, cut them in half and you have twice as many. Get it, Girlie, get it?"

Darnella said, "No she don't get it, Galen. Girlie, if you cut a worm in two then it can still live and . . . Galen, will you stop this nonsense?"

The street lights were far behind now, and they were walking by the light of Galen's flashlight. He was prancing around so much it made staying on the narrow little sidewalk a real chore. He laughed again. "Girlie, I'm a laugh and a half and a ton of fun when you get to know me, right, Darnella?"

"Galen, tell Girlie about the midget at the carnival."

"Well, Girlie we got a midget out there that can fit into a teacup. . . ."

"Girlie, don't believe him. This ain't no fairy tale; this is a real midget like Tom Thumb. She's thirty-five-inches high and weighs about seventy-five pounds. You ain't seen nothing until you've seen her. Galen's got me a job tomorrow, it being Saturday and a big crowd expected. I'll be taking tickets for the midget. Maybe you could come down later in the day, and I'll let you through to see her."

"I'd like that. I really would," Girlie said. She thought about it the rest of the way to Darnella's. She didn't work on Saturdays for the school wouldn't allow it, her being underage and all. Her job was really supposed to be part of her schooling, else she wouldn't have it at all. Tomorrow she would do everything she could to be helpful to Darnella. She hadn't meant to be a burden at Rose's, and she'd have to be very careful not to be one at Darnella's.

When they finally got to Darnella's little place, that wasn't much bigger than a chicken house, Galen shined the flashlight on the door step and then started on in.

"Just a minute!" Girlie called. "There was some money there, didn't you see it?" She bent over and started picking it up. Galen was roaring with laughter.

"Go ahead and count it. You'll find it's exactly thirty cents. Two dimes, one nickel, and five pennies. Everyone picks it up and brings it to me yelling 'Look what I found,' and I tell them they didn't find nothing 'cause it wasn't lost. I figure it this way. If the money is still there when I get home, then no one has come prowling in my things. If it's gone, they probably took it and run like crazy and still didn't prowl in my things. So it's really a cheap guard."

Girlie left the money and went on into the house. She saw the outlines of a cot on the porch and dropped Clark Gable on it. Darnella had lit a lamp in the front room. Galen was already stretched out across their big bed with his shoes kicked off. Darnella was pumping some water at a wooden sink.

"Girlie, let me tie your hair up in rags. With a pretty dress like yourn, you need some curls in your hair."

Galen said, "Oh, Girlie don't look so bad the way she is. It's your sister Coleen that looks so ugly you'd think God turned her wrong side out."

Girlie sat down and let Darnella wrap piece after piece of hair on a rag, and then tie the ends of the rag into a knot to hold it in place. While she sat there, she read the long row of yellowed comics that had been cut from papers and pasted on the wall. Darnella put her own hair up in pin curls, for she had a permanent. Girlie wished that she had been one of Mama's pretty daughters. She thought that she might spend one dollar of her twenty-five and get herself a permanent too. . . . But a whole dollar? It was too much.

Galen yelled, "Cat got your tongue again, Girlie? Come here if you want to see something interesting. Ever see a toe like this?" It looked like Galen only had four toes. The middle toe touched the big toe, but hiding underneath was the second toe all small and pale, with a really long toenail on it. "I'm going to write to Ripley's Believe It or Not, one of these days. Bet he'll take my toe and pay me for the right to put it in the paper. Hey, Girlie, what you want to bet that I can't eat an apple in two bites? Not a little one; a good-sized one. Throw me an apple, Darnella."

Galen ate the apple in two bites. It was awfully late, and Girlie didn't want to hear any more things tonight. She figured she better end it right now. She said, "Galen, what do you want to bet that my hands can reach wider than yours?"

"You name it. I'll take you up on it," he said.

"If I win, I just want to go to bed right off, okay?"

"Got you. Put it there." Galen spread his hand wide right before her eyes. She put hers over his, and her little finger stuck out an extra inch farther than his.

Darnella burst out laughing. "Good night, Girlie. You can turn down the spread on the cot and it's ready. Galen, you ought to stop anyway. We got to both get up and go to work tomorrow."

A large bug was thudding its wing against the screen of the porch. Her tiredness and Clark Gable's purring had her sleeping in no time.

Her tiredness was not entirely gone when she was awakened by Galen and Darnella shouting at each other to hurry. She got her dress on fast and went to help them.

"Darnella, don't we have no milk?" Galen had a bowl of dry corn flakes on the table before him.

Darnella sort of whispered, "You didn't leave me no money."

Girlie tried to think of something helpful. She remembered a fancy sign in the store window across from where she worked. It showed a bowl of cereal with peaches in it.

Sitting on the table was one of Mama's glass bowls, which was Darnella's inheritance, and it held some canned peaches. Quickly Girlie spooned some peaches on Galen's cereal.

"What in thunderation? What's got into you?"

"I saw it in a picture. I thought it might make it taste better."

Darnella took the cereal and peaches and began eating them herself. "Thanks. They taste good, Girlie. Galen is a bear first thing in the morning. Galen, I'll give you a bowl of plain peaches, and you can have a piece of light-bread with it."

Galen soaked the slice of light-bread full of peach juice, gulped it down, and ran out the door with Darnella fast behind him. Darnella called back, "Girlie, you rest up and then come to the carnival, hear me?"

Girlie took Darnella at her word. Since the cover on their big bed was just thrown out and not really made up, she'd rest there. She'd make it right later, but first she sprawled out on the marvelous big purple, blue, and green peacock that was embroidered on the middle of Darnella's pink chenille bedspread. Clark Gable lay at the foot purring and breathing deeply. With each breath his tummy would rise to full roundness and a few loose hairs would fly off into the air. Hot weather was shedding time. Girlie raised an arm to trace the feathers of the peacock, but became more interested in the pattern already traced by red marks left on her arm from lying on the chenille. The marks would go away. All things were temporary, mosquito bites, scratches, bruises, chenille markings . . . didn't matter. Things have a way of disappearing or healing.

One day Papa would want her back. One day he would

say, "Come home. We need someone to figure and help with the farm. We need good cooking and chocolate pudding once in a while for a special treat. You're the one to do those things. You're your Mama's good daughter for sure."

Chances are by the time Indian summer was over, and she'd have to walk three miles from Darnella's place in the cold to attend school, Papa would say, "There's no place like home; come on home, Girlie."

Darnella loved pretty things. By the door there sat a big chalk dog painted all yellow and orange and white with gold glitter on it's collar. Imagine using a fine carnival trophy like that as a door stop! It might get chipped. But it wasn't. Darnella took care of everything she ever got.

Girlie got up off Darnella's bed and went out to the little screened-in front porch to the cot. Even the floursack bedspread that Darnella had made for the cot was starched stiff and draped with perfect evenness as she made it. It touched the clean scrubbed floor boards of the porch.

Darnella had placed a mirror of an old dresser up against the wall of the house, in front of the window, so as to give privacy. She had tacked a board below it, sort of like a dresser top. Another starched flour-sack skirt was on it. And yet another skirt encircled a nail keg, making a fancy vanity stool. On top of this vanity sat a big red piggy bank. This was made of chalk too, of course, but it had sprays of silver to make it shine pretty. Girlie pushed the pig way back until it touched the mirror, making it look as if she had two pigs instead of one, and also to make sure the pig didn't get broken. Darnella was so protective of things. For that matter so was Galen.

He never had a steady job, only worked when someone

needed him. That was regular enough during cotton chopping and cotton picking time; other times there were only short things like the carnival. So they never had any great lot of money, but you'd never know it to see how pretty Darnella kept their little two-room house.

Well, she'd better get some work done for Darnella. First she washed the breakfast bowls and spoons. Then she stripped off the bedding to make the bed up right. Darnella had taken Mama's feather tick, and it took some real shaking and turning and fluffing to make it billow all nice and pretty. Heaven knows Darnella must not have turned the bed right, for there was a comic book stuck under it. She'd have found it if she'd really shaken the tick.

Girlie stopped for a moment to see what comic book it was and. . . . Quickly she closed it and then opened it again to see if she saw what she thought she saw. The drawings were of naked people. And their private parts were right out in the open, drawn big and . . . ugly. They were beating. . . . She closed the book and ran outside. She came back in and grabbed Clark Gable and ran out again.

"I've got to think. Oh, Clark, what am I going to do? That book's Galen's, I know it is. I can't let them know I seen it. Darnella would die. Oh, Clark, I want to go home to Papa. I can't ever look Galen in the eye again."

She would have to leave and that was that. First she made the bed look just the way they had left it. Then she stuffed all her belongings back into her pillowcase. She kept out the ledger, so she could write in it:

There are some things too bad to say out loud. There are some things almost too bad to think about.

92

She took out the three dollar bills that she had earned from cotton picking at Molly's. She wrote a note for Darnella:

I have gone home to Papa on the bus. Girlie & C. G.

She stopped long enough to cut some holes in a box with her knife. She put Clark inside and walked to the bus stop. The bus took her all the way to Sand Hill Road, and from there she walked the four and a half miles to Papa's. She waited in the front room until he got in from work. She tried hard not to remember the pictures she'd seen. To help her forget, she practiced what she'd tell Papa.

But when Papa came in the back door, she forgot every word. "I had to come home, Papa. I was staying at Darnella's and something horrible happened."

Papa walked quickly over to her. "What was that?"

"I was making their bed to help out, and I found an awful ugly comic book. I knew you wouldn't want me around trash, and Mama wouldn't neither, so I came straight home."

For a minute she thought Papa was going to smile the way the wrinkles around his eyes creased up. "And how did you manage that? Did Darnella get you a ride?"

"No, she doesn't even know I left. I took the bus with my cotton picking money. I don't think I'll ever face her or Galen again, I feel so awful. I feel just creepy, Papa. I feel. . . ."

"Now, Girlie, take it easy." Papa's big hand rested on her shoulder.

"Please let me stay home. I can cook for you. Even Molly says I have a talent for cooking. And I can pay my own way. I've got twenty-five dollars."

93

Papa's hand tightened its grip. "From who? Where'd you get twenty-five dollars?"

"I got it from Mr. Hobler for my dress pattern. He's going to give my dress back in a couple of weeks. I'll have to get word to someone to get it for me. It's that pretty yellow dress Mama made me. He give me twenty-five dollars and this new dress for the pattern."

Papa stepped away from her. He just stood there as if he had lost a fight, his shoulders all slumped and weary. "Mr. Hobler, you say?"

"Yes, and he knew me, I mean he knew who I was. He knew Mama."

"Yes, he knew your Mama," Papa said. "I'll hitch up the horses again and take you back to Lil's."

To Lil and Symond, Papa simply said, "Girlie's got a story to tell. Here's her belongings. She's got her cat."

Symond left to quiet Bobby and to leave them alone. Lil was lying down for she was feeling weary from carrying the baby. Girlie whispered her story, except for one part, and she wouldn't say that at all. "Come on honey, tell me," Lil coaxed.

"No, Lil, even if you whisper a dirty word, it is still dirty."

"Girlie, honey, listen to me. The same fire that warms our house in the winter and that cooks our food can burn our house down, if it ain't used right. The special private love of married folks is good, honey. Why there's even a book at the library that tells of its warming nurturing side. You don't have to be any more scared of that awful book than you are when you've seen a house burn. Just know it's something you can prevent. Love ain't cruel nor ugly. Remember what I'm saying."

Girlie said, "I'll try, but that Galen is no better than a

94

big hairy gorilla. I don't see his love nurturing Darnella. In fact, I hope Galen roasts in hell!" She stopped. What had she done? She herself had said a bad word.

Lil said, "Now, Girlie, we got no say in Darnella and Galen's private lives. We got to think what's best for you right now. I sure hate to see you miss out on town school. And you were just plain lucky to have that job. . . ."

Girlie forgot she hadn't told Lil about selling her dress pattern to Mr. Hobler. When she told it, Lil at first was highly interested, but then turned pale and as quiet as a snow bird.

"Oh, Lil, I can't miss out on seeing Mr. Hobler in a couple of weeks. Maybe he'll buy some of your patterns, too. You're nearly as good as Mama was."

"Yes, Girlie, I know. I know. Above all else, you need to hold on to that job. Lovey! That's where you can go, to Lovey's. She's in the country, but I know for a fact they're bussing in the kids around her place to Poplar Bluff. Symond can go over to the Matties and give Lovey a call on that telephone."

After Symond left, Lil explained how it would be the best thing, the very best thing. Girlie agreed with her. What else could she do? Any place was better than the last. Any place at all, now that she could not go home to Papa again. After today, she had to believe that Papa simply did not want her. At that thought, she knew she could cry right in front of Lil if she didn't get outside. So she ran.

Bobby was playing with Clark Gable. She sat down near them. She watched a long line of green, yellow, and orange butterflies nestled close together as they sat on a moist spot where someone had thrown out some wash water. Clark Gable sent them all flying. Then he stalked

95

something in the tall grass, only to come leaping out, shattering a dandelion in full fluff as he sprang.

Next day, Lovey and her husband Frank came driving up in their Ford V-8 with a fancy rumble seat.

Lil gave two loaves of fresh light-bread to Lovey, and then went back and brought out two more for her to drop off at Coleen's as long as she'd be passing near-by anyway. "It was nice seeing you again, Girlie. Have you had a chance to get to the library in Poplar Bluff yet?"

"Not yet, but I will. I surely will."

seven

THE Ford coupe zipped along at least sixty miles per hour. Girlie pressed her back against the opened rumble seat, and clapped her hands tight over her ears and closed her eyes.

Lovey shouted, "Slow down, Frank. Slow down. If you don't care whether you kill yourself or me, at least think of Girlie. I just lost my mother. This family doesn't need another funeral to attend." Lovey's voice took on a different tone of scolding as she added, "Girlie, uncover your ears and open your eyes and act civilized. Frank's been driving for four years now and ain't never killed a soul. Look how them telephone posts have rotted off at the bottom. No wonder we can't hear a body on our new phone with them posts just swinging loose on the wires like that. Girlie, if you're going to be so all fired scared, crawl up in front with me. Frank, slow down, and let her up here with me."

Frank yelled, "I can't slow her. She shimmies when I drive slower." He jerked to a stop and Girlie forced her scared body to move up and over the side of the rumble seat. She had barely touched her right foot to the running board when Frank took off again at sixty miles an hour. Lovey jerked her on in and slammed the door by reaching across to hold one hand on the steering wheel while the other pulled the door. It wasn't easy, for Lovey was fat and occupied most of the front seat.

Frank was yelling, "Let go my steering wheel! Hold on, Lovey! Grab onto her, Girlie. Hey, you got in all right. There now, that wasn't so bad, was it?"

"You didn't kill me that time, Frank, want to try again? You driving like a demon and the inner tube's full of patches." Lovey was mad but within minutes she was grinning and wiping her hair back from her face and joining Frank in a lively yodel. "Yo-ho-lā-i-he-e-e-e-e!"

Girlie wasn't at all sure that this place was going to be much better than Darnella's. She sat wedged in on the hard edges between Frank and Lovey's seats. Clark was under her feet in a little box, yowling for all the world to hear. She'd cut holes in the box with her knife, so lack of air wasn't his problem. She could barely hear him, for a high-speeding car makes its own racket. That, added to the yodeling of Frank and Lovey, was enough to keep her mind off everything.

Lovey stopped yodeling and yelled, "Girlie, want a stick of chewing gum?"

Girlie nodded yes, and tolerated the elbow punching and shoving around that Lovey gave her while hunting for her pocketbook. She finally found it under Clark's box. The gum was Spearmint. Pretty soon she cut out all the other noises and gave her attention only to the sound of the crackling of her chewing gum. "Chomp, chomp, crackle, SNAP." She kept the rhythm intact, and they all made it home safely.

Home was a tall, skinny white house and a little red car shed. Down the path was a piece of a gray barn without a speck of paint. It was rotting away at the bottom, much as the telephone posts that Lovey had pointed out. The house wasn't big at all, once you got inside. Frank and Lovey showed Girlie the whole downstairs. It was only a kitchen and living room and one tiny bedroom.

Frank said, "Me and Lovey took this bedroom. It's tiny but it's cozy. That's the way we like it, don't we, kid?" He gave Lovey a big hug, and added, "You got the whole upstairs all to yourself. There's the stairway that leads to it."

The stairs, which were only two feet wide, went up from Frank and Lovey's little room. As she looked up toward the tall peaked loft at the top of the stairs, she could see that there was no ceiling; just open rafters.

But when she went up, it wasn't bad at all. Spider webs softened the dark wood and played in lovely patterns from one projecting nail to another. Right in the middle of the loft room was a single bed with the prettiest yellow quilt on it that Girlie had ever seen. Lots of little picture girls with long dresses and sunbonnets marched hand in hand all across it.

Girlie caught her breath. Lovey was right behind her, pushing her the rest of the way into the room.

"I thought youd like it. See, Frank, I told you she'd like it. Coleen made it. She give me a little silver bracelet once for getting her over to Fort Leonard Wood to see Jack. Later she made that quilt, waiting for Jack. I told her, 'Not even Mama ever made one that pretty. Then she mentions my bracelet she give me, and I know she wants to trade, so I took it. I thought maybe one day I'd have a kid, but you're my kid now, ain't you, Girlie?"

Frank said, "Now, Lovey, don't put the girl on the spot like that. No, sir, no one ever made a quilt like that. Coleen's got talent enough but you have too in your own way, Lovey, and the Lord's going to increase it ten times, or my name ain't Frank Bowls. Girlie, answer me this, what could we do with a cot-sized sunbonnet maid quilt when we only had a regular size bed in the house? We needed you to come use our cot up in this fine room. I set it up quick when Symond called."

Frank was laughing and Lovey was, too. She gave him a shove that made him prick his finger on a roofing nail that was sticking through on the low slant of the roof. He sucked the blood from his finger and laughed all the louder. Girlie couldn't feel scared or strange or not wanted anymore, with all that laughing going on. The only thing she could possibly do was join in and laugh too.

"Girlie," Frank said as he got a very serious look on his face, "I don't want to tax your brain too much, nor cause you to lose any sleep tonight, but I got a thing for you to puzzle over and give me an answer come morning. What kind of quilts or covering did the folks in the Bible use? Go ahead, use your Scriptures if you have to. You'll find some in the drawer of that trunk. They're yours. Yours to keep."

Girlie saw the trunk then. It was nestled back under the eaves, all brown to match the wood of the roof, but the buckles had once been gold. They were discolored and tarnished brown now, almost the same as the wood. She lifted the rounded lid, and there was a tray or sort of an open drawer in the top, and in the middle compartment

100

was a small Bible and next to it a stuffed doll. A sunbonnet doll to match the ones on her quilt. She picked it up and touched it softly to her neck, before she realized she was too old for such.

Lovey said, "Now, *that* I made myself. Got two of them extra quilt blocks of Coleen's and fixed a doll of them."

Frank said, "Now I don't like that, don't like that one bit. Lovey, she likes that old doll you made more than the Testaments I give her."

He was laughing again. Lovey too. Girlie laughed with them. It was a way to avoid words she guessed. She didn't have to get all choked up or to think of the right thing to say or anything. She just had to laugh like Frank and Lovey.

Lovey wiped her eyes because she'd laughed so hard she was crying. She caught her breath and tried to settle down. She sputtered, "Bring the doll on downstairs if you want. We all got to eat and I got to get off my feet. They're so swollen now that they look like a couple of stuffed toads." Lovey laughed again and Frank too. But Girlie didn't see anything funny about Lovey's horribly swollen feet.

Frank said, "Stuffed toads. Boy, I can just picture you walking with two big green stuffed toads for feet, and then croaking with every step. Girlie, you ever see a stuffed toad? There's another little thing for you to ponder. Where in the Bible does it mention toads?"

They followed Lovey as she squeezed back down the narrow stairs and went into the kitchen. Lovey set out a plate of cold bacon, and Frank cut the light-bread that Lil had given them.

Lovey said, "Frank you're going to have to run Coleen's bread over to her tomorrow and I'll send her a half of cake. She don't eat enough to keep a bird alive and hardly ever bakes for herself with Jack gone. I couldn't live without my sweets. I crave them just as bad as Mama did. Though I think sweets is the cause of Mama having big babies that ripped her up something awful. You weighed thirteen pounds yourself, Girlie. Boy, you was a cute one with the longest black hair a body ever saw on a newborn. Guess I ought to be thankful for not having to have big babies, but I ain't. I'd take them, too big or not. Rose has a kid and Coleen's pregnant, and their husbands gone all the time. Frank's here at home, day in and day out, and me with nothing to show for it."

Lovey howled with laughter and Frank swallowed his bite of sandwich, half choking and joined in with her.

When they'd finished laughing and finished eating, Frank handed Girlie the scraps and said, "Here, feed your cat and my dog."

Girlie jumped up in a panic. "You got a dog?" she cried, running to look for Clark Gable. She found him on the front porch curled up sleeping. Not four feet away lay a big old brown long-eared hound.

Frank was right behind her, laughing again. "Had you scared there for a minute, didn't we? Yep, we got us a dog now. Figured when we moved to this place, we ought to have a dog. Got him from a family that owned cats. I knowed he wouldn't hurt your cat. Never has laid a tooth on a cat, but take rabbits, now that's a different story. Boy, can that dog catch rabbits!

"I've never had to waste lead shooting since I got him. And squirrels. . . . Law, he has them before they know it. We had a mess of squirrels when Lil and Symond come to visit. Lovey can skin a squirrel faster than any woman I know. Real talent she's got. Bobby said she was pulling

102

the squirrel's overalls off when he saw her skinning one. Now wasn't that cute? Bobby's a mite slow, but we'd take him and love him to pieces if we had a chance."

Girlie fed the pets and went back inside. Lovey was leaning against the cold cookstove washing dishes. She said, "I ever tell you how me and Frank got together? He took me to a pie supper. It was the first time he ever asked me for a date. He walked me all the way to the church without saying a word if you can believe it. He bid four dollars for my pie which was three dollars more than the highest bid. But some crazy boys was laying for him to do just that. They'd snuck my pie out to a barn and altered its filling with you know what. Oh it was a sight, and the smell was worse than rotten, but that's when Frank's real self showed its ears. He just busted out laughing. I knowed right then I was going to marry him. Any man that can handle a situation like that and laugh is the man for me."

Frank put his arm about Lovey's big waist and said, "I guess I was just born lucky. It's a fact, Girlie, I was. I lost my glasses in St. Francis River once and had not a penny for new ones. I'm blinder than a mole without my glasses, but you know what? Next day when I pulled up my trot line, I'd caught myself my own glasses and three catfish besides. The Lord always seems to provide a ways and means. My, we're mighty happy to have you staying with us, Girlie. But I'm afraid we've just about wore you out. Better get on up to your bed."

She found Clark Gable and did just that.

The next morning Frank woke her up with, "Rise and shine, Girlie. I already been over to Coleen's and back, and that was slow going. Got stuck in a rut behind a Sunday driver, had my car shimmying up an earthquake before he finally turned off. Girlie, Lovey ain't feeling any too good, and I wondered if I could get you to turn the cows out to pasture. That would be a good job for you to do on a regular basis. You can ride Ole Jersey when you bring them in at night. She might buck a little, but I'll 'spect you'll be plenty tired after going to school and working in the store and having to catch the late bus. Least ways, it'll put a little excitement into your life and be a big help to us too. I use to ride cows when I was a boy."

So Girlie turned the cows out each morning thereafter, and rode Ole Jersey home each night when she got off the late school bus. The bucking never once made her drop her schoolbooks and usually had her laughing over her tiredness when she came in the door to the smell of Lovey's baking.

She'd gotten used to the new school and the ways of the town kids. She'd found the library and discovered it was full of fact books as well as story books. She was doing so well at her work that Mr. Krendall was trying to talk her out of going on to high school for he wanted her to quit and work full time. She'd taken courage from Mr. Hobler's enthusiasm for her ideas. In D.O. sales class she made out a list of baby clothes for farm women that were reasonable, practical, and pretty. Mr. Krendall let her sell them at a little off the regular price. The word got around and lots of farm women came to her for their needs. Mr. Krendall was pleased, and let her calculate some cost and do some ordering on her own.

Mr. Hobler came back in two weeks like he'd promised and returned her yellow dress. Pinned to it was a little note saying:

*This dress has made a hit at my company. I wish we
had more new patterns of this kind.*

                                        H. Hobler

She told him again about Lil cutting out nice patterns too,
and he promised to keep that fact in mind.

All in all, things went well enough that Girlie didn't let
herself dwell on the fact that Papa had not let her come
home. Lovey was a different sort of woman than Mama,
but she was nice, very nice. Girlie was only too happy to
help her in any way she could. Sometimes Lovey would
have her take eggs along to school in a lunch pail and
then on to the store when she went to work. She gave
them to Mr. Krendall in exchange for yard goods, buttons, and thread. Christmas was creeping closer, and
Lovey was busy making Christmas presents.

It wasn't a common practice to exchange gifts, but
Lovey said it was to be their first Christmas without
Mama, and she just felt like doing something special for
everyone. Girlie helped with the sewing, making mis-
takes sometimes like sewing one of the pants legs of
Parker Jr.'s little suit with a French seam and the other
leg with a plain seam. Lovey laughed, but she made her
do the plain one over.

Girlie helped, too, with making applesauce the shortcut
way, by throwing in whole apples and cooking on low heat
until the skins popped open and then running the soft
mess through a sieve. Frank did his share too. He put a
pile of black walnuts that he'd picked on a plank, and ran
his car back and forth over them to crack the shells.
Girlie picked out the nuts to add to their cornbread. At
the end of each wash day, she helped by folding the sheets
that never lay smooth, because they'd been hung to dry

over Lovey's big lisle underdrawers to hide them from the sight of the passers-by. They all worked together, busy and happy.

Finally, after Lovey had tucked in a scrap of material and some patching thread with each present made, the gifts were ready for Christmas. Nita, along with Wanda and her husband and little Susy, came down from St. Louis. Coleen's and Rose's husbands were home too. They all met at Papa's. Even Galen came along with Darnella.

Frank said to forget Galen and his hidden book and just to pray he'd get up out of bed earlier, so he'd make a better living for Darnella. If he got up three hours early, it'd make an extra month's work in a year's time.

Anyway, everyone acted happy and friendly. Everyone laughed a lot. Everyone was careful not to mention Mama too much. Then all the sisters went back to their own homes. Papa didn't ask anyone to stay on, even though he was getting quite thin on his own cooking.

Right after Christmas, Lovey's health took a turn for the worse. Frank said she overdid it with all those presents she made. Girlie offered to stay home to help, but neither of them would hear to her missing school or her job. Lovey struggled along as best as she could by working a spell and resting a spell as Mama had always had to do. But in early April on Girlie's thirteenth birthday, Frank had to drive over to Doniphan to get his mother to come help out.

Girlie stayed home from school that day so that Lovey wasn't left alone. "Here's some cold water," she said and placed a large tin cup next to Lovey's bed. "Anything else you want?"

"Yes, there sure is. I want you to sit down and let me talk to you. Frank's Mom is coming, and I think you was too little to remember her when you saw her last. I figure I better give you fair warning. I guess you might call her an ugly woman. She's got a nose as long as I've been sick, and she has worse eyes than Frank, but she wears pretty clothes. You can't help admiring her for not giving up on life. She's a hard worker too, worth the whole kit and caboodle of all the pretty women in the family put together. So, Girlie, treat her like a friend, because that's what she is."

It wasn't hard at all to act friendly to Mrs. Bowls. She jumped from the car, a bright red flash in her pajama-legged pants. The flare of the legs was so wide, the hem came up as high as her waist when she caught the bottoms to keep them out of the mud.

The minute Frank brought her in and introduced her to Girlie, she slapped her on the back and said, "Why, I know this thing. Sure I know her. You're Mary's baby, ain't you? Well, I'll say this. You were the cutest baby I ever saw, and I'm the best of judges." She laughed a hearty laugh and continued, "Your hair was five inches long and you weighed thirteen pounds and a little extra when we slung you on some cotton scales to weigh you."

"I don't remember you, Mrs. Bowls. I guess I was too little even if I was a *big* baby." Girlie felt good at making her own joke and giving reason for laughter.

"Sure you remember me. I was there helping your Mama when you were born, but that ain't the last time I saw you. You must have been about three years old when your Mama had another bad sick spell and called on me to help out. I remember when I came in, there you sat with a yellow cat in your lap.

Girlie didn't say anything. She could never remember any other cat than Clark Gable.

107

Mrs. Bowls dropped her chatter and walked up to Lovey's bed and stared at her for a long time. "Well, you've got yellow jaundice or you've got tuberculosis by the tone of your skin."

Lovey raised up as if to get out of bed.

Mrs. Bowls pushed her back down and ordered, "Now you stay there. You may be stubborn as a heifer, but when I'm here to run things, you'll stay in bed. Frank, I think you better call in Dr. Lester."

Lovey said, "No. No, my Mama never give up nor give in. She didn't go running up doctor bills either with every little pain she had to bear."

"Lovey, relax. Frank, go get Dr. Lester on the phone. I'll talk to him. Lovey's still trying to please her Mama. I tell you a dead mother has more power over her children than a live one."

Girlie went to the kitchen to start supper, and washed out the soured milk from the straining cloths Lovey hadn't quite got put away before she had to give in to go to bed. Mrs. Bowls' voice was shouting loudly into the phone in the other room. "Okay I got you. We'll see you in the morning when you make your rounds." Soon she was in the kitchen again saying, "Girlie, let me finish the supper. You go find me some sassafras roots and some spicewood. You know what that smells like."

Frank came in to assure his Mom, "Sure Girlie knows. She's got a snozzle like a hound. If she's smelled it once, she'll know it again."

Girlie said, "I know the smell of spicewood and I'm sure there's a tree down back of the cow pasture by the river. Don't forget to add more water to the beans when they boil low, Mrs. Bowls."

She found the sassafras roots close to the railroad track

and the spicewood twigs on the tree she'd remembered.

Some watercress grew in a pool of water back up from the river a way. She stopped to pick some and to get a drink. Watercress grows only in pure cold spring water. She took it all home. Along with the herb tea, Lovey had a good supper of beans, watercress, and cornbread Mrs. Bowls made. She had added walnut meats to it like Girlie did, but also a good bit of sorghum. It was delicious. Then came the surprise. Mrs. Bowls brought out a birthday cake with thirteen candles for Girlie to blow out.

She cried a little from pure pleasure, and they all laughed at her. Then Frank took Mrs. Bowls home. It was a long way but Frank said his mother needed a decent bed to sleep in and he didn't mind.

The next morning, Mrs. Bowls got a ride back over with Dr. Lester who was full of talk along with his doctoring. The minute he came in the door he said, "Well, howdy, Girlie Webster. How's your Papa? Last time I saw him he was getting so skinny he looked like he'd been kept a prisoner in a war. I told him he was going to kill himself if he didn't stop smoking, but he's still rolling them I noticed. Well, he's the one that'll be pushing up daisies, not me."

Then Dr. Lester hit Frank in the belly and said, "Frank, you want to stay healthy, you better get rid of that pot."

"Nope, not on your life." Frank pulled back, mocking fear of Dr. Lester's slap. "That pot has cost me a few thousand dollars, I figure, and I aim to keep it. There's been a lot of hogs and beans and corn gone into the making of it."

The train whistle blew, letting everyone know the time of day. Girlie went to the window to watch. The steam from the engine billowed high in the air. "It's getting cooler out, ain't it, Dr. Lester?"

"A bit I guess, but long's it's not cold enough to freeze the seat of my britches to the car seat I don't notice. I did see lightning. Better be expecting an electrical storm. We had a dilly of a storm the night I brought you into the world, Girlie. That was a night and a half. So much electricity in the air I was shocked to see your Papa and your sisters all with their hair standing on end. I guess mine was no different, what I have to stand up. You had hair enough though. Thought we was going to lose your Mama for sure. But, she pulled through and lived another dozen years which proves I ain't quite God yet. But it's aggravating to give people advice and see them turn their ears the other way. Lovey, you plan on doing what I tell you or not?"

"I'll try, I'll try."

"Well, I'm telling you to stay off your feet for two to three months, live mostly on the teas I prescribed, and beef broth, and some lean beef now and then for strength. Absolutely no sugar. I'll make you out a prescription. I'm thinking that your symptoms is headed toward diabetes.

"Don't act so surprised. Think back to what Nellie Winshaw and Gerty Mattie was like before they suddenly got skinny and had to start insulin. Frank, you want to have to give Lovey shots everyday? You want that, Lovey? I know what I'm talking about. Had your Mama cared to come back to me for a checkup I'd have told her about what I'm telling you, Lovey. I figure from the looks that she had the early stages before she died. Which just gives *another* reason she should have listened to me and not had that last baby. I told her it'd kill her. My diagnosis was right. Only my timing was twelve years off."

"I can't stay off my feet for two months. I got a home to keep."

"You make the same sounds your mother made. I'm asking you to rest and start eating right. Guess you come by things naturally, stubbornness from your Mama and poor eating habits from your Papa."

Girlie resolved to make an entry in her ledger:

Habits are inherited. My bad temper must come from Papa, since Mama never got mad.

Dr. Lester was still ranting, "Now listen to me. I'm a doctor. Everybody runs out of tomorrows sooner or later. Mrs. Bowls, can you stay here and make her obey me? Look at her, swelled as big as a stuffed toad right now." With the mention of stuffed toad the seriousness broke, for Frank and Lovey started laughing, and Girlie joined them.

Mrs. Bowls screeched, "It's not such an impossible request as to set you hee-hawing about it. I'll stay. I'll be happy to stay."

Dr. Lester snapped his bag shut. "Fine. I thought you would. You got more sense than the young ones." He quickly scribbled a prescription. Frank took the paper, squinted his eyes trying to make out the words, then handed it back to Dr. Lester. "Write it so I can read it and understand it. If I'm going to give my last dime for medicine, the perscription is going to be one I can read." Dr. Lester rewrote it.

Frank paid him and let him out the door. "Now there goes a happy man because he knows we're going to do as he says, right, Lovey? Why, he's so happy I could hear the money jingling in his pockets. Well, if you're going to need beef, Lovey, I better see if I can get my credit with

111

Stockman's extended and buy a steer to butcher."

Mrs. Bowls said, "You'll have to take me to pick up the rest of my clothes and close up the house for a spell. But that can wait a day or so I reckon. Where do you want me to sleep?"

It was quiet for a few seconds and Frank laughingly said, "In a bed of course. You sleep right here in bed with Lovey, and I'll make a pallet in the front room. Now we got that settled, I'd best go on over to Stockman's."

Girlie knew what they were thinking and were not saying. They needed her bed, but they would never ask her for it. "Frank, you have to go right by Coleen's. Could I maybe ride along for a visit?"

"Sure you can. You need to get out of this sick room for a minute. Want to come with us, Lovey?"

Mrs. Bowls was swatting at him. "Get out of here and stop heckling my patient."

Frank ducked and ran saying, "I hear you, woman." Girlie grabbed her ledger and ran for the car too. As soon as they were in the car, Frank said, "Girlie, you been reading your Scriptures? Tell me what man in the Bible was commanded to listen to a woman. I'll give you a hint. It's in Genesis."

Girlie smiled at Frank for trying to clear the air, but she said, "Frank, you'd never take the five dollars I get from the store, told me to save it for an emergency. You better take it now for the beef. I have my twenty-five dollars from my dress pattern for an emergency. It'll be my paying for some of the food I already ate. It's rightfully yours anyway, same as it would have gone to Parker and Rose or to Galen and Darnella. Here take it."

Frank moved uncomfortably in his seat.

"Don't say nothing until I'm finished. I come with you because I aim to start living over at Coleen's. Mrs. Bowls can take my bed. Coleen will take me until Lovey gets well. I know she will. But I got a favor to ask, would you and Lovey keep Clark Gable? I could never take him to Coleen's."

"Sure we'll keep your cat. I'd never allow you to take him over to be swallowed up by her vicious hounds! That crazy Shep of hers would eat a cat or anything else. That dog has some appetite. . . ."

"Then it's settled. And you'll take the money for the beef?"

"Girlie, I think you mean it and I think you'd be broke up if I didn't go along. I can use it for a fact." He took the money and stuck it in the pocket of his overalls. He sang "Oh, Righteous Day" until it was time to drop Girlie off at Coleen's. She was greeted by three big vicious looking dogs that Coleen had got to keep her safe while Jack was in the army. They would kill a cat for sure.

Anyway, Girlie asked Coleen what she'd come to ask. First, she explained about them needing her bed over at Lovey's, and that she didn't have any other sisters left to go to. She'd not be home an awful lot, for she'd catch the early bus to school and get the late one home after work. She'd pay her the five dollars for room and board.

"Why don't you go home to Papa where you belong?"

She couldn't tell Coleen that she was never going to try again to go back to Papa. She would never again ask to be shoved away.

"Papa don't want you. Is that it, Girlie? He never had too much of liking for me either because I wasn't born pretty like Rose and Lil and Wanda. Maybe that's some of your problem, Girlie. Anyway, I'm not afraid to say a

113

thing if it's so. I guess you can stay here for the time Lovey's sick and down. She never done me no harm. Jack won't be home from the service before then anyway. He'll get out in June. I bet him I'd have strawberries ripe and ready for his first meal home."

"Thanks a lot, Coleen. I'll go with Frank now and I'll be back later with my clothes."

Mrs. Bowls and Lovey both threw a fit when she told them, but they never stopped her.

Lovey said, "I'm sorry, Girlie. I'm too sick to fight, I guess. If I was skinny as Coleen I might look as sick as I feel. Papa never understood or believed Mama was as sick as she was. Sometimes when I feel like this, I'm glad that Mama died. It was so hard on her to live for years in sickness and pain. The Lord did right in taking her."

Mrs. Bowls agreed, "Yes, it was a blessing the Lord took her. She wasn't one to want to live being useless. She always earned her keep. Fine woman. Girlie, you come from a good woman and don't forget it."

Later that night at Coleen's Girlie carefully wrote in her ledger:

Dr. Lester told Mama not to have me or she would die. I don't want my Mama or Lovey sick but I don't want them dead either.

Then she added the entry about habits being inherited.

eight

Except for missing Clark Gable and Lovey and Frank, things weren't so bad at Coleen's. Girlie caught the same school bus and everything else was pretty much the same, all through the day.

The biggest change in her day was, Dobe Tyler suddenly seemed more interested in the fact that she was a girl, than the fact that she was good at math. He was around wherever she went. He followed her to the library and looked for books in the stacks next to where she was looking. It was sort of nice to have his attention, but she didn't dare search around in amongst any more fact books for fear he'd find out what facts she was searching for. Anyway she was almost convinced she was going to have to look in the grown-up's fact books for more information. She'd read everything Mrs. Grossmeyer, the librarian, had for children.

Dobe even sat behind her and watched her eat her

mashed-bean sandwiches. Coleen wasn't all that good of a cook and Girlie had little time for it. She made sandwiches from leftover beans or potatoes, and loaded them with mustard. She missed Lovey's peach butter and blackberry jam for sandwiches. Dobe must have had an appetite like Coleen, for he didn't eat much. He just stared at her. She wasn't pretty like Rose or Lil, but he didn't seem to know that.

A week after she'd moved to Coleen's Frank's car come chugging along. He'd brought Clark Gable in his box so she could say hello to him. He brought over half a beef liver since liver couldn't be canned and would spoil before they could eat it.

Frank also brought news of Lil's new baby. "It's a girl, and as bald-headed as a peeled apple, Symond said, but bright-eyed and cute as a whistle. She come a little early, but Dr. Lester said there was no worry."

Coleen sat there with her little silver bracelet bobbing back and forth on her skinny wrist as she quilted and listened. Girlie kept waiting for her to speak up with the same excitement that she felt. But Coleen didn't say a word, so Girlie talked. "It's just what Lil wanted. She wanted a little bright-eyed girl. Lil told me so herself. I bet she ain't mad at all that it came sooner than she expected. She was having trouble carrying it—I mean her. What did they name her?"

"Pansy because they said she looked just like a little soft flower. And they give her the middle name Mary after your Mama."

Coleen stuck her needle securely into the double wedding ring pattern and pushed herself back from her quilting frame. "I'm hoping my baby don't come early. It's not supposed to be here until after Jack gets out of service. I don't know what I'd do, me here without a phone or a car to get help."

"You got me," Girlie told her. "I could cut across the fields and get Mrs. Bowls to come. Frank could bring her back in the car fast enough, couldn't you, Frank?"

"Of course I could, and I would. Any time you need my car, you're welcome to it too. You don't have to stay in this house quilting and pining your heart out for Jack's return. You want to get out and go visiting, just let me know the day, and you can borrow my car. All I ask is that you bring it back with as much gas as you started out with."

"I would like to see Lil's baby girl," Coleen said.

"Why sure you would, and so would Girlie. I tell you what. Sunday I'll bring the car over, and you can drop me back home and go visit all you want. Promise me one thing, you'll stop and tell Lovey all about little Pansy. She does love babies and staying in that bed all day, everyday, is wearing on her. I love that woman, purely. Don't act shocked, Coleen. It ain't no crime to talk of loving someone. God never said we had to wait until a person died to open up."

"We'll be glad to stop and tell Lovey, won't we, Coleen?" It was aggravating that Coleen took so long to speak up sometimes.

"We'll be glad to talk to Lovey," she finally agreed.

"Good," Frank said. "I'll be over with the car bright and early, might even get here before breakfast. Girlie, go say good-bye to your cat, and I'll take off."

She said a quick good-bye to Clark Gable, and Frank

drove off at a high speed. Nothing was in Girlie's mind now but Lil's baby. It would mean breaking into her emergency money but she was going to buy something from the baby clothes she sold at the store.

It took the rest of the week to decide, but finally she bought a thin little receiving blanket with blue puppies and pink flowers on it for thirty-five cents. Then she bought a yard of soft pink flannel so Lil could sew for her little girl. She showed both things to Coleen to get her approval. Coleen was not excited.

"I guess a body would like to sew for her baby. I guess it would be nice having new material," was all she said.

Frank let Coleen drive him back to his house to see if she knew how to handle the car. She did, for Jack had taught her when they dated, but Frank had to keep reminding her to keep it up to sixty. Soon as she let Frank out, she took it back down to thirty, and the car shimmied constantly for the rest of the trip.

Coleen pulled a fast one. She was heading down the road that led to Papa's, not Lil's.

"Don't ask me what I'm doing, Girlie. He's my Papa, and I can stop and see him for a minute if I want to. We'll still be going to Lil's." There was nothing Girlie could do to stop Coleen, so she just sat silent and waited.

Papa was certainly surprised to see them. First thing Girlie noticed was how much Coleen and Papa looked alike, now that Papa was so skinny. Being big can surely alter who you favor. Girlie didn't care to talk to Papa after last time, and she made no motion to get out of the car. Coleen hopped out right away.

Papa said, "What brings you two over?"

Coleen said, "Nothing much. I just came to find out why Girlie ain't staying home with you where she belongs?"

"Now, I don't see as how that's any of your business, Coleen."

"It is my business when I'm the one that's keeping her. I'm the one that has to worry if she's fed, worry if she gets sick. I ain't saying I won't do it, but I am saying that I need a reason why you ain't doing it."

Girlie wanted to hide her face for Papa was red-mad, and she was afraid he might hit Coleen. That'd be awful. Papa didn't strike. He just rounded down to that weary beat position and stood there for awhile. Then his head shot up, and he looked Coleen in the eye and said, "I meant to spare any of you knowing. But if you've got to know, go ask Lil. She can tell you." Papa turned and walked rapidly back to the house.

Coleen yelled at him, "I'll do that. I'll just do that!"

Girlie didn't dare ask one question of Coleen, even though she would have liked to ask a million. More than anything she was amazed that Lil knew something that none of the rest of them knew. It wasn't like Lil to keep secrets from her. Coleen drove sixty-five all the way to Lil's. She was the one that was shaking now instead of the car, and she was still trembling when they stopped. Girlie wanted to offer her a steadying hand, but she didn't dare touch her.

Bobby came out the door screaming, "Girlie, come see what I got. I got a baby."

Girlie had to say this for Coleen: She controlled herself real well and oohed and aahed over little Pansy. Then she got around to asking Lil what Papa had given her the right to ask. Girlie held her new little niece and listened.

"Lil, we just come from Papa. He says I'm to ask you why he's not letting Girlie stay home with him like he ought to. He says you know, and he says you'll tell me."

Before Lil had looked weak and happy; now she looked weak and scared. "I guess I have to say it. Girlie, honey, maybe you'd rather not hear it."

Girlie held little Pansy close and tucked the new blanket in smoothly. "I aim to hear it, too, Lil."

"Papa has always doubted that Girlie was his girl. He was up North picking peas nine months before she was born, and she was a full-term baby, there was no doubt about that."

Girlie got up with little Pansy and walked to the back door. She stood close to the screen with her back to her sisters, and she let the tears spill out. Papa didn't believe he was her Papa. Oh, how she hated him! She lost herself in the hate until she was no longer aware that she was in Lil's yeasty sweet home. She stood there until little Pansy started screaming, and Coleen touched her shoulder and said, "Frank and Lovey will be expecting us. We got to go now."

Lil kissed her good-bye and said, "Girlie, honey, Papa loved Mama. I know he did. He'd lived with her all these years, always wondering."

Coleen snapped, "Not to mention that Mama run his house and kept his kids. Pretty ones, ugly ones, she took care of us all."

Later in the car speeding back to Frank and Lovey's, Coleen said, "Well, that explains why he buried Mama on Sand Hill. She was an evil woman who wronged him."

"She was a good woman. My Mama was a good woman. Mrs. Bowls even said my Mama was a good woman!" Girlie was shouting, but she didn't care.

Coleen said, "She was my Mama too. I never said she wasn't a good woman, for I know darn well she was. I don't believe she even knew how to do wrong or had the time for that matter. With raising nine kids, she didn't have time to find another man." Coleen was roaring with crazy laughter.

Girlie saw that horrible comic book of Galen's flash before her mind, and she screamed, "Stop it. Stop it, Coleen! Don't you ever mention this to me again!"

And Coleen didn't. Not another word did she say the rest of the trip, and not a word was uttered at Lovey's. They told only of Pansy and Lil. And not a word did she say back at Coleen's. Girlie was left alone to read and reread her ledger and try to think everything out.

After a few days, when she was ready to face the next question, she asked it. If Papa was not her real Papa, then who was?

nine

GIRLIE thought of every man she had ever known and she was absolutely sure that none of them could have been her father. She'd just have to go to the library and get a fact book on heredity. She'd have to make the most of her time, too, for school would be out in a week. She'd have no way to get to the library after that.

In the file catalog she found Heir, Heirlooms, Legal Estates. Mrs. Grossmeyer greeted her, "Well, hello again, Girlie. Can I help you find something?"

Girlie stood there for a moment. She didn't quite know how to ask for a book on heredity. What if she pronounced it wrong? Sometimes she could read a word a long time, pronouncing it in her own head, only to find out later it didn't sound like that at all.

Finally she just said, "I want a book about . . . about, well, about how a baby gets their brown eyes from their parent who has brown eyes." Papa's eyes were blue, but

Mama's eyes were brown, and the girls were about evenly divided. Only Girlie had black eyes. "But I want a book that really goes into it."

"Of course, Girlie, I'll bet I have what you want. We're fortunate to have this book. It was quite an investment, but I'm sure it's going to be worth it. It's being used a lot already. Sit at the table over here. I'd better carry it. It's pretty heavy. There. It's the complete story of life: birth, death, heredity, you name it."

"Heredity. I want to know about heredity," Girlie let the name come out in the same way Mrs. Grossmeyer said it. She'd been saying it almost right all along, and she felt pleased. The book was so fat it would take her forever to read it all the way through, so she looked for an index and, sure enough, it had one.

She read lots of things about heredity. The more she read, the less certain she was about anything. There were so many things that could make a body turn out the way it did. It did sort of explain how she could look so different from the other girls and still be their sister. But it didn't give her any definite idea as to what her father *had* to look like.

She thanked Mrs. Grossmeyer for letting her read the book. It was too big to check out and carry home on the bus, so she left the library empty-handed which was a good thing. No sooner did she step outside than a pebble came sailing her way, and she had to dodge. It was Dobe following her again. It made her feel good that someone in this world thought that much of her. She hurried on to work.

About a half hour before quitting time, Mr. Hobler stopped to see her again. His smile was pleasant. His teeth were real even and white, without a trace of tobacco stain on them. She liked him and smiled back his greeting. "Miss Webster, nice to see you again. I see you're still getting a lot of wear from that lovely yellow dress. Let me tell you a story about that dress. You know I copied the pattern?"

"I know. I still got twenty-four dollars and ten cents from it."

"If you stay that thrifty, you'll be a millionaire one day. Well, that dress has made money for me too. It has been my very best seller! What do you think about that?"

"I think you ought to get my sister Lil to make you another pattern. She's almost as good as Mama at cutting patterns. I told you that before."

"Indeed you did, and I didn't forget. That's what I wanted to talk to you about. Your mother had a rare talent. I believe you have inherited your mother's taste and also have your own special sense for design. If your sister has come by that same talent, then I'm definitely interested." He smiled and added, "And you calculate the cost since you seem to have a talent for figuring too."

Girlie could hardly listen to his last words. What was that he said? People inherited talents. She'd known that all her life. "Nita will sing alto same as Mama or Lovey one day. Coleen quilts like Mama. Russel can't do figures same as Malford. Don't know who Girlie gets her talent for figuring from." Oh-h-h, she could hardly look at Mr. Hobler. He had known Mama well, and he had the same knack for figures and business that she herself had. Was this man her Papa? Hair and eyes were exactly the right color. Oh-h-h. No wonder he had given her so much money for the dress pattern. The more she looked and thought, the more upset she became.

Mr. Hobler was still talking, and she hadn't heard a

word he said. "Miss Webster, is something wrong?"

"My name's Girlie. I'm not Miss Webster."

"Well, all right, fine. Girlie, I was saying. Is there some way I can get in touch with your sister Lil?"

"She won't want you giving her money on account of Mama."

"Believe me, child, I would never do that. I didn't *give* money to your mother. The fact that she needed it in no way took away from the fact that she earned every penny I ever paid her. That was fourteen years ago. Before you were born, in fact. I lost contact with her. You can imagine how happy I was to find you working right here in the store. Now, is there . . . Miss . . . Girlie, are you all right? I'd better call Mr. Krendall."

Mr. Hobler left to get Mr. Krendall, and that was threatening enough to make any of the store help straighten up. She put her thinking on straight again and was smiling when she saw the two men coming back to her. Mr. Hobler wasn't her Papa. What an absolutely silly thought! He was a very nice man who wanted to get pretty dress patterns, because that was his business. My gosh, she'd almost caused Lil to lose out on a chance to make some money by her silly, crazy thoughts.

Before either could say a word, Girlie said, "Mr. Krendall, I'm fine. I guess I was hungry. I went to the library today instead of eating my lunch." Why, that was the truth, what she'd just told Mr. Krendall. So she really was weak. No wonder she'd had such silly thoughts.

Mr. Hobler said, "May I get you something to eat? I take businessmen in the city out to lunch. I don't see that it's any different if my business happens to be with a nice young lady. Mr. Krendall wouldn't mind letting you off fifteen minutes early now, would you Krendall?"

Mr. Krendall agreed so fast, you would think he did things like that all the time. Mr. Hobler guided Girlie to the little restaurant across the street and told her she could have whatever she liked to eat. She chose a hamburger, on a yeasty bun with pickle and mustard and onions.

She said, "It's delicious! Tastes like I always imagined a hamburger tasted, only better." He bought her a second one.

She gave Mr. Hobler Lil's address so he could write to her, and she promised him she would never skip lunch by going to the library at noon hour.

She really wanted to go back to the library the next day to look at the big book again. She decided to eat her lunch as she walked to the library. Dobe came up beside her, eating his lunch too. "Hi, Girlie, want an apple?"

The apple looked good. Apples never kept year round on the farm, so she never had one except in season. But they could be bought in stores. Town kids were lucky that way. "I'd like it if you'll hold my lunch bucket so I can peel it."

Dobe was happy to do that. Girlie took her little knife off her belt and peeled the apple. "Papa is real good when it comes to peeling apples. He can go all the way around one and not break a peel."

Dobe said, "That's a talent! That's a real talent."

"Hey, I did it. I didn't break the peel once!" Girlie held it up for Dobe's admiration. Papa had a habit of slicing off pieces of his fresh peeled apple and sharing them with his girls. Girlie sliced off a piece and stuck the tip of her knife in it and handed it to Dobe. He thanked her and thanked her. Thanking her for a piece of his own apple?

126

She didn't make an issue of it, for they'd come to the library and had to be quiet.

She took her lunch pail from Dobe and walked away from him to find the big book. She got Mrs. Grossmeyer to carry it over to the table for her again. It wasn't that she herself couldn't carry it. My gosh, she had lifted a good-sized pig once, when it got stuck in the fence. But she didn't want to take any chances on dropping this beautiful book and tearing it.

She didn't know what to read today, but decided to read about birth since Lil had a brand-new baby, and Coleen was going to have one pretty soon. She found out that birth was an interesting, and sometimes a very complicated thing. Some babies are born too early, and some too late. The early ones, like little Pansy, may not have any fingernails or eyebrows or hair on their head. Lil had been lucky. Some babies have been known to go as long as a few days to a month and a half overdue. Overdue babies may be big and have quite a growth of hair on their heads. Girlie stopped reading.

She'd heard it and heard it, "You're the one that had the long hair. You weighed thirteen pounds and then some. Hair a good five inches long. Longest hair I ever saw on a newborn." She herself had been an overdue baby! Papa *was* at home with Mama *ten* months before she was born! She'd known all along that Papa was her real Papa. She was so happy she picked up the big book and went running with it to Mrs. Grossmeyer.

The librarian took it from her hands as it grew heavy. "I'll check it out. I'll check it out!"

"No, dear, this book can't be checked out. I'm sorry, I wish I could let you take it, but it has to be left here for

127

reference. So it's handy when others need it."

Girlie didn't know what to say. She felt disappointed and hurt and dumb. She ought to have known better than to think she could check it out. She was just a stupid country kid. She sat back down at the table and opened it to the important place again. She'd have to get one of the little pieces of paper from Mrs. Grossmeyer and copy the words. She'd have to show them to Papa, so he could think straight and relieve his mind of doubt and worry.

It wouldn't do any good. Papa would think she made it up. He'd think that first because he never believed anybody or anything until he checked on it himself. He wasn't likely to come to the Poplar Bluff Library. Second, because Girlie had been known to sort of not tell things exactly as they were. She had a habit or used to have a habit of leaving out a few things sometimes, in order to. . . . What could she do?

She wished she had a camera. She'd take a picture of the page. Then she could take the picture to Papa. But no one in the family owned a camera except for Uncle Bob who only came down from Minnesota every year or two to visit.

She had to have that page. She just had to have it. Books don't print lies. Papa would have to believe it if he saw it in a book printed all neat and pretty. Papa would say, "Girlie, you've done me the biggest favor of my life. I've been suffering unduly all these years. I can't thank you enough. You'd better come home where you belong. Your Mama was set on you going to high school, and I aim to keep you so as you can go on and get educated."

This little bit of writing meant everything in the world to her. She had to have it. If she had it, she could go home to Papa right now.

She was crying. Tears that had waited for a long time. Tears of relief. If Papa had only had this little bit of writing, he wouldn't have buried Mama up on Sand Hill. Through tears she took the little knife off her belt and carefully cut the important writing out to take to him. She'd not even go to work. She'd get the bus right away and go home. But she couldn't. She didn't have her money with her at school. She would have to go to work first, and then to Coleen's on the school bus. And then it would be too late to catch the highway bus. She'd have to wait until tomorrow.

It was not until she reached the store that it hit her what a terrible thing she had done. She had cut Mrs. Grossmeyer's fine new book. She felt weak from the awfulness of the thing she had done. Maybe another girl would need to read these very same words, and they would not be there. She left the baby-clothes counter and went to look for Mr. Krendall. "I got to go out for a few minutes."

He looked at her, shook his head and said, "Okay, go eat. But I'm warning you, one more time of your skipping your lunch, and you'll be out of the program. Now, Girlie, you're a valued employee. This is your last week unless you're ready to reconsider my offer. As long as you're a student, they'll not let you work summers, and you underage. But if you decide to quit school. . . . Anyway, I want you to know. I'm not running a business where my help can come and go as they please. Hurry it up."

She ran all the way to the library. She ran straight to Mrs. Grossmeyer and handed her the piece cut from the book. "I want you to put it back. I took it and . . . I sinned. I don't know why. I'm sorry I took it, Mrs. Grossmeyer."

"I knew you took it, Girlie. I saw Dobe looking at the book after you left. He was very surprised that you had done such a thing and I must admit, Girlie, so was I. I'd never have expected that from you. The book will have to be replaced."

"I know. I'll bring you the money tomorrow."

"Girlie, I'm sure you don't understand. The book cost us fifteen dollars and fifty cents."

"I'll bring you the money tomorrow." Girlie said it again and left. She went back to the store and finished her day's work and caught the late school bus home to Coleen.

Coleen was excited. "I've got three strawberries just fat to busting. They'll be ready for sure when Jack comes home next week.

The thought of Jack coming home was too much for Girlie. She was supposed to already have been back with Lovey by the time that happened, but Lovey wasn't on her feet yet. Frank had told her a couple of weeks ago that Dr. Lester wasn't sure how much more time it would take. She knew she'd not be getting the five dollars to give to Coleen for room and board, but had told her she'd pay her out of the emergency money. Now she must give most of the emergency money to the library for the book. She'd have to tell Coleen.

"Coleen, I have to give the library fifteen dollars and fifty cents for a book that I cut something from."

"You did what?"

"I found this book that told that some babies go overdue up to a month and a half and get real big and have lots of hair like I did and. . . ."

Coleen held her hands across her large stomach. "I sure hope my baby don't go overdue a month and a half, for

Jack will be gone back by then. I never heard tell of any going that long. I don't want to have a big baby like Mama."

"You're not getting the point, Coleen. It means Papa is my real Papa!"

"'Course he is. I never thought he wasn't. He's the only one that thought that. Why'd you say you cut up that book?"

"So I could take it and prove it to Papa."

"Girlie, that shows a lack of good sense. You know better than to tamper with public property. People get arrested for such as that. Nobody ever cuts stuff out of a book. That's a downright sin. Mama'd roll over in her grave if she knew you'd cut on a book. It may be hard on you to part with that money of yourn, but you got no choice."

"But that money was supposed to be for you, for my room and board, until Lovey is on her feet."

"You'll have to do what's right by the library first, and then you better start thinking on getting some kind of work if you can this summer. I ain't mad. I guess I don't have it in me to be mad with Jack coming home. I'd sort of hoped we'd be here alone, but I understand and feel sorry for Lovey. After all this sickness, she may never get that baby she'd like to have."

"Maybe she could adopt one. Some people do that. There is a chapter in that book I cut, about adoption." A wonderful thought came to Girlie. If she paid for the book, then it would be hers to keep. She would give it to Lovey. Lovey could lay there in bed and read up on adoption and, well, just everything. And, she could take the whole book and show Papa. It was worth the money. She

131

felt happy again for the first time since the cutting.

"Coleen, yes, ma'm, I bet them strawberries will be ripe by the time Jack gets home."

Actually the strawberries were ripe by the last day of school, the day before Jack was due home. Coleen didn't pick them, said she'd leave them to get dead ripe, and for Jack to see them on the vine. The last day of school was really only going back for report cards and graduation diplomas.

Rose and Darnella were willing to let bygones be bygones, and both of them showed up to watch Girlie walk through the eighth-grade graduation exercises wearing the red satin blouse Lil had made for her. Coleen didn't want to leave the house, just in case Jack came in a day early, but she'd given Girlie the prettiest little quilted purse you could imagine. It had the same double wedding ring design, only smaller, of her big quilt she'd gotten finished for her and Jack. Girlie thought Coleen had just been making another quilt block. She hadn't expected any fuss at all, certainly not a purse.

After the graduation was over, Rose came up and handed her a package. "This here's from Wanda and Nita, they sent it to me to bring over. Hey, don't open it so fast; it's private."

Girlie peeked in the end she had opened. It was a pair of fancy pink panties with lace! They were too pretty to hide but, of course, she'd never let a soul see them.

Darnella handed her another package. "And this is from me, Molly and Lovey and Rose put together. Better just peek at it too."

It was a pink satin underslip with lace and a little embroidered rose right in the center of the neck. It was a wonderful thing to feel loved by so many sisters. She plainly didn't know what to say. So she just said good-bye as Darnella and Rose left with the rest of the visitors to go home.

She still had a little time left before her last day of work at the store, so she went to the library to see if Mrs. Grossmeyer had the new book she'd ordered yet.

"No, Girlie. I told you it takes awhile to get a book order through. Want to see how nice I scotched that piece back in? Say, you look right nice in that red blouse. Red looks good on you with your dark hair. Now I know this book means a lot to you, and I'll bring it out to your place when the new one gets in. Draw me a map how to get there. It's all right; I enjoy driving in the country."

She didn't know how Mrs. Grossmeyer knew what that book meant to her for the librarian had never pried in to see why she'd done what she'd done. She drew the map and said good-bye. She'd just have to hold her patience and wait until she got the book before she thought again of going to show Papa. The job she'd like to have this summer would be helping Papa on the farm.

She finished her job at the store that day, and Mr. Krendall said he'd hire her again next year unless she changed her mind and decided to skip high school and get right into the business world where the money was.

The school bus was almost empty since many of the students had ridden home with their parents. A couple of the kids who were on the bus began singing, which started the others singing too. Girlie clutched her gifts to her and sang joyously. Her spirits were so high, she almost got home before the bus did. She skipped across the back field to Coleen's singing all the way. Coleen came out the door and yelled, "What in the world is going on, Girlie?"

Girlie had plopped down on a stump near the garden to watch the dogs romp. It was a perfect day. Even Coleen seemed to feel it, for she came out with a light blue bandana on her head to protect her hair from the wind. It matched her dress. A pretty starched apron protected the dress, too. Her shoes were polished, and she stopped to dust away a spot that had gotten on them when she'd turned too fast. She sure was ready for Jack to come home. Girlie smiled.

"My strawberries!" Coleen screamed suddenly. "You ate my strawberries!"

Girlie ran over to the bed. Sure enough, the strawberries were missing. "I didn't eat them, Coleen. I swear I didn't touch them."

"Then who did? They were here this morning when I showed you, and here at noon when I checked to see how they were bearing the sun. Girlie Webster, there ain't been but two people on this place today, you and me."

"I didn't eat them, Coleen."

"Just you and me, and Lord knows I wouldn't ruin Jack's treat and lose my bet. Girlie, I think you're lying to me. Your library lady might let you off scot free with letting you have the right to buy a book that you ruined and nothing more, but it won't work with me. Them strawberries meant a lot to me."

"Coleen, I wanted you to win your bet with Jack. I ain't lying to you. I wanted you to win, even if Mama did say it was wrong to bet. I wouldn't never eat your berries. I know you been tending them and waiting, and waiting and tending."

Coleen's thin fingers gripped Girlie's arm. "Some of your actions lately don't make good sense. Well, I'm telling you right now that I'm going in my house and pack your belongings while you go over to Frank's, and tell him I want to borrow his car. We're driving to Papa's. He ain't unloading his responsibilities on me. He's the one that got you into this life, and he can face up to raising you. What really gets me is to see you lie like that, without a trace of guilt on your face."

"Coleen, I didn't eat your strawberries. It'll be getting dark before long, and you oughten to be driving Frank's car."

"I'm going to drive it. I'm going to *talk* to Papa right now before Jack gets home. I got a right to my own life. I got my own home to make. I got my man to please and to plan for. I'm new at this. I'm having my own babies, my own little girl. A girl that would weep with guilt if she was caught lying. Look! Look there at the juice on the ground. Ain't even had time to dry up."

There was certainly strawberry juice on the dry ground. Small specks of seeds and bits of berry clung to the dampness. Now who could have done it?

The thought came to Girlie that once Mrs. Dorsey tried to commit her husband to the asylum, and he was so clever that he had them believing it was her that needed to go. Coleen was awfully filled with anxiousness and obviously was mixed up as a person could be. If Mama were here she'd say, "Girlie, you can't talk to her right now, that's for sure."

It wasn't exactly the way Girlie had planned it, but she guessed she'd be seeing Papa tonight. She could tell him of the facts she'd found and tell him she'd get the book to him as proof later. Maybe this would be enough for right away. She could stay on with Papa, and Coleen could come back and get herself settled down and wait for Jack.

She ran all the way across the field to Frank and

Lovey's. Even if Coleen were worried and anxious and addled a bit, she ought not have accused her of lying. She hadn't lied once since Mama died, not even when she had cut the library book. Poor Coleen was awful lonely for her husband. Maybe she should have talked to her more. She'd best convince Frank that the thing to do was to humor Coleen.

Frank understood as soon as she explained things. He said, "Now, you stay here and visit a minute with Lovey and tell her all about that graduation of yours. Tell it good now, Girlie, so's she'll feel she was right there. I'll get Coleen settled. It won't hurt you to visit your Papa tonight. Tell him you graduated. Ought to make him proud."

Girlie told Lovey about the graduation and the big library book, and how maybe she'd be staying home with Papa after all. She boxed up Clark Gable to take him along just in case. Coleen thought that was a good idea. She said Papa was going to find out she meant business. Frank told them to remember the headlights and reminded Coleen not to go over sixty-five or under sixty.

It was almost dark by the time they got to Papa's. At first it looked as if no one was at home. No one answered their calls. The bed in the living room that Papa and Mama had slept in was stark empty, not a stitch of bedclothes on it. The house was full of clutter with boots and work jumpers and dirty socks laying about. The smell of Prince Albert and soured dishwater filled the air. Coleen didn't look so determined anymore as she stood in the midst of the mess calling softly, "Papa. Papa." Girlie started picking up the dirty socks, and Coleen hung up a plaid work shirt that had both elbows missing.

Dad's voice came from upstairs where the girls had once slept. "Who's down there?"

"Papa, it's me, Coleen. I brought Girlie back home to you."

"I can't hear you. Give me a minute." Girlie could hear Papa coming down the stairs. "That you, Coleen?"

"Yes, Papa, I brought Girlie home." Papa came into the living room. He heard this time and wasn't happy about what he'd heard. Girlie would have known that, even if his face had been clean shaven and all spiced up for Sunday, which it certainly was not. With his whiskers long and showing more gray than black, he looked mean, not just mad. For a moment Girlie wasn't sure that she wanted to convince this mean Papa that she was his daughter.

But Papa's looks seemed only to give Coleen new determination. "Papa, I brought Girlie home where she belongs. Girlie thinks she's got proof that she's yourn, but I don't care whether she's got proof or not. She's got your name, and whatever happens to her will reflect on you anyway. The law says you're responsible for her, not me. Girlie has taken to destroying things and lying. I'm bringing in her things, and then I'm going to my own home."

Coleen ran out the door before Papa had time to change the expression on his face.

Girlie quickly started explaining to Papa what had really happened. "I didn't lie. I didn't eat her strawberries. I swear I didn't, Papa. I paid for the library book. Mrs. Grossmeyer is going to bring me the book I ruined, so I can prove to you that Mama carried me a long time overdue. That's why I had all the long hair, Papa. The book said that some women has carried babies as high as ten and a half months. Even if Mama just carried me ten months . . . my birthday is. . . ."

"I know when your birthday is, Girlie."

Coleen tossed Girlie's pillowcase into the room. "Girlie, I set Clark Gable loose out in the yard. If I was you, I'd clean up this place first thing and do my talking later."

With those words, Coleen left. Girlie ran after her and shouted, " 'Bye, Coleen. Don't forget to turn on the headlights." Coleen might have been going over sixty-five when she pulled out in Frank's car.

When Girlie came back into the house Papa had a lamp lit. He said, "Girlie, sit down. Now. . . . It's a fine trait to be wanting to uphold your Mama's name, but saying something's possible and saying that's the way it actually was, is not the same thing. You're young, and there's a lot of things you don't know or can't really understand if you do know. Nita had a fair head of hair, as far as that goes. Not that I want to argue any points with you. Soon as I get my shoes on and get a lantern hunted up, I'll be taking you over to Lil's."

"Papa, you need me." Girlie threw her arms wide so that Papa would see his own mess. "I oughten to go to Lil's. Papa, she can't stretch her pennies any further than they already are with another baby there. I need you, too, Papa. I ain't got no more sisters to take me in. Please Papa. Even if I ain't your daughter, let me come live and work with you? Some folks take kids when their Papa *and* Mama is someone else. Couldn't you sort of adopt me, too, Papa? Don't you like me? Am I that bad a person?"

"No you're not bad; you're a good girl," Papa said.

He didn't look at her when he spoke again. "I ain't got nothing against you, Girlie. It's just that my mind is set . . . been set for a long time. Now, cut out all this talk and go find your cat."

Girlie found Clark Gable hiding out in the corner by the smoke house, a spot where he used to sleep a lot. She didn't bother with the box with the holes in it. Clark Gable wasn't scared of riding in wagons and, besides, she needed the comfort of holding him. She didn't talk to Papa all the way over to Lil's. And Lil didn't ask questions when they got there.

She just said, "You know where to put your things, Girlie. Pansy's still sleeping with us, and Bobby's still in the big crib, so your cot is still yours."

Girlie fell asleep smelling the fresh yeast growing in the night.

ten

THE next day as soon as Symond was off to work and Bobby fed and outside, Girlie sat down to talk to Lil while she nursed little Pansy.

"Lil, it seems just like Papa don't want no proof that I'm his. Is it because I'm so bad? My temper and all?"

"Now, Girlie, you know you're not. Look at all the fine things you do. Papa don't want proof because then he would have to bear a load he can't bear. Papa didn't want you born, nor for that matter did Mama. Now, Girlie, honey, don't be shocked. I figure they didn't want a good share of us, with times as hard as they've been."

"But they didn't *have* to have us!"

"Girlie, you're so young. They didn't know how not to. Mama didn't find out until a man told Papa about letting love take its course only at certain times of the month. That was when Mama was so dreadful sick after having you. At least Mama didn't have any more, and she was alive to raise you until you become a fine, capable young woman."

"If Papa and Mama couldn't help having us, then they couldn't. It ain't nothing for Papa to push me away about."

"Now, Girlie, think. You read that new library book. You know that no two people *have* to have children. But if they choose to love, then with it goes the chance of children and the responsibility to raise them. I got Pansy by chance, though she's precious to me."

"I'm not very precious to Papa."

Lil busied herself changing Pansy from one breast to the other and tucking her blanket in to cover her neat little toes.

"I think maybe you are. But Papa's burden is a big one. If he had held back from loving Mama, then you would never have been born and Mama would not be dead. That's a big burden for a man to bear. . . ."

"I didn't cause Mama to die! No, no, don't say that, Lil. Mama didn't die because I was born. Dr. Lester said she pulled through. She died from something else. Something dreadful that people whisper about. She didn't die because of me!"

Lil didn't say anything. Girlie wished that she would yell back. She wanted to fight with Lil and make her admit her words were wrong. But it was no use. Girlie went to look for Clark Gable, and Lil did not call her back. She found Clark and then she got out her ledger and reread all the facts. She picked up her pen to record the new facts, but she couldn't bring herself to write them.

Finally she went back to Lil, who had finished feeding Pansy and was washing the breakfast dishes. "You mean that Papa caused Mama to die?"

141

"No, honey, I don't think that, but Papa does. I think it's the way of life, and life ain't always simple or easy. But Papa knew the chance, and he also was possessed of feeling like we all are. So he figures he is the cause unless. . . ."

"Unless what, Lil? Whatever it is you know we got to tell Papa."

Lil laughed a sorry kind of laugh and pushed back the dishpan. "Papa already found the unless, honey. A desperate person thinks ten times faster than the rest of us. Not knowingly, of course, but they come up with ways and means to keep on living with themselves."

"Unless what, Lil?"

"Dr. Lester told Papa at the time Nita's birth wrecked Mama's insides that he knew of no way to repair the damage. He told Papa another baby would kill her, that she must never get pregnant again. She did but she was lucky enough not to die right away, as Dr. Lester thought. But she never really recovered from your birth. Papa would have to accept the fact that he had a hand in Mama's death, unless you wasn't his, Girlie."

"But . . . but I am. I got proof I am . . . well, almost proof I am. He knows Mama wouldn't look at no other man."

Lil had started washing dishes again. She didn't look at Girlie when she said the next words. "Papa knows that another man praised Mama highly for her talent. He wasn't comfortable with that. He forbid her to sell that man another pattern, when Mama had a hundred needs for the money."

Girlie ran from the house again, over the fields and down to the river. She sat on the bank, letting her head sway from the weight of the knowledge it contained. Even

142

Lil thought she might be the daughter of Mr. Hobler. But Lil loved her.

Oh, how awful to cause the death of someone you love! Oh, poor Papa, what a burden. She knew how Papa felt. She, herself, wished it had been Nita who was the last one born. What a terrible wish!

Girlie got up and tossed some dried bark at some water bugs. They scattered. She threw more and more things into the water until the bugs dashed about like gnats near a lantern. Then she waded into the water's edge and tried to catch a water bug in her hand. It was impossible but for a long time she tried. At last she stopped her game and allowed herself to think about Mama and Papa again. And to think about herself.

The fact was that she might or might not be Papa's daughter. Lil had not tried to reassure her. Why didn't Lil say, "Girlie, honey, I know you're Papa's as well as Mama's daughter. You take after Papa in. . . ." But she didn't take after Papa. Not in his ways, except in temper, and not in his looks. She took more after Mr. Hobler than she did Papa. Girlie started to throw another stick into the water, but held back and continued figuring on things.

Even if she was Mr. Hobler's daughter, he didn't know it . . . at least she didn't really think he did. Anyway, he hadn't raised her; hadn't peeled apples for her; hadn't bought her a penknife or a fountain pen; hadn't told her she cooked right well; hadn't played with her on the floor or let her sit beside him when he hauled melons. She didn't give a hoot who her real Papa was. She absolutely did not!

She was herself: a fine mathematician, a good cook, and

the best help that Mr. Krendall had ever had at selling baby clothes. She was a girl raised by Mama and Papa. She could get by in this world.

She'd go back right now and tell Lil she'd be working at the dry-goods store full time and not going to high school. She'd rent a room for herself in Poplar Bluff. Somehow she'd persuade a landlord she was old enough, same way Mr. Krendall planned to convince the authorities to permit her to work. It was hard to tell a body's age when they got past twelve, and she did look pretty grown up. She walked back across the field to Lil's.

That was Papa's wagon in front of Lil's! And that was Papa talking to Lil and Bobby. She didn't really want to see Papa right now. Her thoughts were too new. She'd not want to cry or act up in any way. She wished he hadn't come.

Papa left them and came to meet her.

"Hi, Girlie."

"Hi, Papa."

For a moment nothing else was said. Then Papa cleared his throat for talking. He sort of turned her around so they started walking away from Lil's. "Girlie, I been thinking. Well, I been thinking almost all the night through. I always did think you had right good sense, Girlie, and what you said about adoption was just right. Of course there's no need for the law, I figure; it would be just between the two of us. Your Mama refused to give you a name, because I didn't right off when Dr. Lester asked for it. She could be a stubborn woman, Girlie." Papa was smiling when he said that. But Girlie didn't have a mind to interrupt his talk. "I was thinking that people that adopt a baby gives them a name of their own

144

choice. I been thinking the whole night for a good given name for you. What do you say to the name of Glencora?"

"It's pretty. I like it. I really do, Papa. I'll take it."

"All right. You're Glencora Webster now for the records. I can write to Jefferson City about it tomorrow. . . . No, I think I'll write as soon as we get back home today."

Without much trouble Girlie had their walking take a turn back toward Lil's. She'd have to get Lil aside and tell her. But Lil had more company. It was Frank's car. Maybe Lovey'd taken a turn for the worse.

She ran ahead of Papa. It wasn't Frank. It was Coleen and Jack.

Symond said, "Coleen's come to show us she's really got a husband."

But, Coleen's first words were: "Shep eats strawberries. I had to come tell you, Girlie. We caught him doing it again this morning. I hated to borrow Frank's car again so soon, but Jack is here to drive, and Frank didn't mind anyway. Lovey's full of life this morning, talking about how as soon as she gets well, she's going to adopt herself a baby. Said that Frank could do his part by naming it. Hi, Papa."

Girlie didn't try to explain what Papa had just told her. She asked, "Where's Lil?"

"In changing the baby's didie, where else?"

Girlie found Lil. "Don't rush, Lil. Stay in here away from the others. I got something I want to tell you."

Lil was smiling. "Papa already beat you to it. He's so happy that he had to spill over. I think you gave him the way out that he was looking for." She put the last pin in and handed Pansy to Girlie.

145

Girlie hugged little Pansy close and ran out to show her off to the rest.

Jack was telling Papa, "Yep, I'm going to buy myself a Ford with my discharge money in September. I like the way they run. I know just what Frank ought to do to take the shimmy out of her."

"Ain't Pansy cute, Papa?"

"She's a girl, ain't she? Can't beat girls. No, you sure can't. Well, Girlie, better get your belongings and cat, and let us scat. We got to get moving. We got work to do. For one thing, I need to start looking for a horse that will get you to high school next year."

"And I got to start teaching you to cook, Papa, so when I finish high school you'll be ready to take care of yourself, and not get thin again if I go off after a big career in retailing or something."

When Girlie tried to get up on the wagon, holding both her pillowcase and Clark Gable, she slipped. Papa reached out to catch her. For a moment his hand lay out in front of hers. What a wide handspan he had. Even wider than hers. Why hadn't she noticed that before? Because he's never been thin before. Papa's skinny hands, hands that were no longer just big hands, showed where she'd gotten her wide span. At least she was thankful to know who her real Papa was. No one else in the whole country had hands like Girlie's! Certainly not Mr. Hobler.

She said, "Papa, would you stretch out your hand . . ." and then she stopped.

She couldn't give him back his burden. She knew what it was to carry a burden of guilt, to wish something had never happened, to desire to undo what had been done. She had been able to right her own wrong by paying for the library book. To make it right enough that the hurt went away. But Papa couldn't make Mama live again. He could never, never make things right.

She started again. "Please stretch out your hand and take Clark Gable for me. He's fussing and scratching. He's awful anxious to go home."

BERNIECE RABE is the author of two earlier books set in southeast Missouri, where she herself grew up: *Rass* and *Naomi* (both Nelson).

Like Girlie, she is familiar with the ramifications of life within a very large family, for she had ten brothers and sisters, seven stepbrothers and stepsisters, and one half-sister. And she remembers well and admires the willingness to try and care for their own, even if poverty and hard times made the coping less than perfect.

Like Girlie, she was very good at "figuring"; at thirteen she won a trophy for excellence in mathematics from the state of Missouri.

She now lives in Sleepy Hollow, Illinois, and has three sons and one daughter of her own.